the Island

CORAL ISLAND
BOOK ONE

LILLY MIRREN

black lab press

Read The Series In Order

CORAL ISLAND

The Island
The Beach Cottage
The Blue Shoal Inn
Island Weddings
The Island Bookshop
An Island Reunion

One

BEATRICE RUSHTON-PIKE GOT MARRIED TOO young. She mused over this thought as she ran a fingertip along the marble bar in the den. It was dust free, and she smiled to herself, grateful for the cleaning crew that'd come through the previous day and scrubbed the house from top to bottom. She and Preston were twenty years old when they tied the knot. And now that their daughter had reached the same age, she shuddered at the thought of how young it really was.

She and Preston had been children only three years prior to their wedding day. Who let them think it was a good idea? She vaguely recalled her mother saying something about them being too young for such a big commitment, and Dad mumbled some gentle words about how a long engagement was often a good choice. But at the time, it'd gone in one ear and out the other. They were in love. And to them, love was all that mattered.

But there was no chance she'd let Danita consider marrying while she was still at university. In reality, she knew it wasn't up to her and there would be nothing she could do about it if Danita chose to take that step, but she liked to cling to the illusion that she still had some sway over her daughter's decisions. Thankfully, Danita had never had a real boyfriend and the subject of marriage hadn't come up, so it wasn't likely she would have to address the issue for a while yet.

Their son, Harry, was a very young eighteen. He'd left for university two weeks earlier and until then still liked to have his mother pack his lunch for school, and take naps on the weekends. It was hard for her to believe he was an adult. Sometimes she still saw those adorable, brown floppy curls and imagined him the happy, uncoordinated toddler she chased around the house hoping he would't fall and hit his head on the furniture.

The house felt so empty now he was gone. He was only one person, but the noise he generated when he was home was enough that she never felt lonely. Now, it was a different story. The house was like a cavern. Every sound she made echoed through its empty halls and bounced off the tiles. She'd never really thought of the tiled floor as cold before, but since Harry left home, she'd found herself visiting carpeting shops to look through swatches. She'd talked to Preston about giving the house a facelift, maybe getting an interior decorator in to redo the place entirely.

He'd simply shrugged and hadn't lifted his eyes from the phone in his hands. "Maybe we should downsize. We don't need a place this big anymore."

His words had saddened her. She didn't like change. And this house was where they'd raised their two children. Should they sell it and move into something smaller right away? Would the kids miss out on coming *home* for the holidays, instead visiting a strange, impersonal townhouse in an overly built-up part of the city?

There were no smaller houses in their neighbourhood, so it would mean leaving everyone they knew behind and starting over somewhere else. Surely he couldn't mean it. But instead of addressing these questions to the side of his head, she ignored the niggling thoughts and decided not to raise the subject again for a while since he'd seemed perfectly content with their sprawling suburban property before she'd said anything.

It'd been twenty-five years ago that they'd stood on that wide, sandy beach on Coral Island and pledged to love each other forever. It seemed like yesterday. She sighed at the memory. So much had happened since then. Was it possible they were the same people who'd made that heady commitment, with their eyes blinded by passion? She felt as though she was an entirely different person, and Preston certainly behaved like one. Sometimes she wondered if she knew him at all. Still, they were both excited to renew their vows. The party was tonight — the perfect way to celebrate their twenty-fifth wedding anniversary.

Everyone would be there. Well, everyone other than Dad, who had made some excuse not to travel from Coral Island to attend the party. He rarely came to the mainland these days. Always had something to attend to. The house needed cleaning, the fencing was broken, the chicken coop had been battered by a storm. And her brother Bradford had made a similar excuse — he had a business to run, he couldn't get away from it in the busy season.

If she wanted to see her father or brother, she'd have to go there. But she hadn't done that in years. And so most of the time, she only saw her father's face over a video call. She missed him.

It was infuriating the way he resisted the idea of travel. He knew how busy she was with the catering and the children, although now that both kids had officially finished high school and were out of the house, she had more time than she had before.

Perhaps it was time to go back to Coral Island for a visit. The thought filled her with a longing for her old home, something she hadn't felt in an age. Could it be that she finally missed the place after all this time?

It would be her birthday next week. Perhaps she could catch the ferry to the island and spend a few days with her father to celebrate. Preston wouldn't mind—he had that sales conference in Melbourne to attend. When she'd suggested she should come with him so they could spend her birthday together in the city, he'd told her they could postpone and enjoy a meal out together when he got back.

She'd hoped he might make more of a fuss over her forty-fifth birthday. It felt like a big milestone, especially now that both children were out of the house. But Preston had never been much for birthday gifts or thoughtful surprises. He was more of the steady, reliable type of husband. At least, that's what she told her friends.

It was true — he'd always been there for her over the past twenty-five years. He was a good provider with his management position in the sales division of a large scientific devices supply company. He'd travelled the world in his role, spending weeks at a time away from the family while she kept the home fires burning.

She nursed their babies. She ferried them to kindergarten, then school. She supervised homework and listened to piano practice. She drove Danita and Harry to ballet and soccer. She went to all their sports carnivals and recitals at school. She'd even managed to build a moderately successful small catering business on the side.

And their hard work had paid off — Preston's job had given them a comfortable lifestyle; she'd never had to worry about money. And now their children were grown and both were generally loving, kind and successful young adults. They could both be proud of what they'd achieved. After twenty-five years of what had often felt like a slog in which they'd barely had time to acknowledge one another, it was finally time for the two of them to kick back, put their feet up, and spend some quality time in each other's company.

The first thing she'd do after this anniversary celebration was book a trip somewhere. She'd always wanted to go to Paris. Maybe they could spend the New Year there. It would be a romantic adventure and just the thing they needed to get back some of the intimacy and passion they'd lost over the years of living like ships in the night.

The doorbell rang and Bea bustled to answer it, wiping her hands on the apron tied neatly around her waist. She tugged the door open. She lived on the outskirts of Pennant Hills, an old Sydney community on the upper north shore with leafy green neighbourhoods and generously sized blocks. Bea and Preston owned one of the largest blocks in their subdivision, and all of the neighbours knew one another well. Popping in for a quick chat was a community pastime.

"Good afternoon, Bea." Nellie Armstrong from next door stood on the doorstep with a casserole dish balanced on one hand and the leash tied to her straining blue heeler in the other. The dog wanted to get in through the front door to search for Bea's pug—she knew it. And she also knew how that would end, with the dogs dashing madly through the house, the blue heeler hot on the trail of the pug whose tail would be tucked between his legs with several items of furniture smashed on the ground in their wake.

Deftly she stepped onto the porch and pulled the front door shut behind her to prevent a catastrophe.

"Hi, Nellie. What do you have there?"

"I made tuna mornay. I thought it might be nice to serve tonight at your big anniversary doo." Nellie smiled, her teeth impossibly white. Her toned abs showed beneath the Lorna

Jane crop top she sported, and her fake tan glowed a perfect shade of bronze.

Nellie always made Bea feel frumpier than usual. She pushed her curly hair back from her face and found it had stuck to her forehead with the sweat she'd worked up moving furniture and baking treats for the party all day.

"That is so kind and thoughtful."

"Are you excited about it?"

"I suppose so. It's a lot of work. I've wondered why I decided to do this to myself about fifty times today. Of course, I should've hired more help, but I love to cook, so I thought it would be fun. And besides, my usual staff are all invited guests, so I didn't want to bother them."

Nellie chuckled. "Cooking is definitely not my idea of fun, but I'm sure you'll do a fantastic job. I can't wait to try everything. Anyway, I must get moving if I want to take a shower before the party. I'll see you then, okay?"

She waved goodbye, and Bea tented a hand over her eyes to watch her go. She was about to walk inside with the casserole when a car crackled down the gravel driveway and parked in front of the house.

Preston was home. And he'd parked in the driveway again. He knew they were having a party and that guests would be using the drive to circle in front of the house. She'd asked him twice already to remember to park in the garage this evening. She sighed and resisted the urge to roll her eyes as he jogged up the stairs in his business suit.

"Hi, honey," he said.

She raised her cheek for his kiss, which he dutifully gave. "Did you have a nice day at work?"

He shrugged. "Okay, I guess. What's that?"

"Nellie brought it over for the party."

A shadow flitted across his face. "Oh, that's tonight. I completely forgot about it. Darn, I'm so tired."

She bit back a retort. How could he forget about their party? Twenty-five years of marriage and a vow renewal. It'd been on her mind for at least six months. She'd been planning for four. And she'd spent days getting the house ready, purchasing decorations and supplies. And all day cooking. It made her heart clench to realise that he hadn't given the celebration a passing thought.

"Oh," was all she said.

"When does it start?"

"Two hours from now."

"Never mind." He pushed a smile onto his face. "I suppose I can work up some enthusiasm, although I really want to talk to you before you get into crazy preparation mode."

She wondered if he really believed it only took two hours to prepare for a party with one hundred of their family and friends attending. And if that's what he believed, how had he managed to get to the age of forty-five without having learned otherwise? She knew the answer to that — it was her fault. She'd taken on the bulk of the work around the home, organised parties, cooked, baked, sewed, helped neighbours and friends, chosen and put together furniture. Anything that needed doing around the house, she'd done it.

She'd undertaken that single-day course one time years ago, the one that helped her identify how she gave and received love. She had discovered that her love language was acts of service. She loved to do things for people to show them how much she cared, and she'd done everything she could to show Preston how much she loved him for twenty-five years. What she'd failed to realise all that time was that he wouldn't notice her effort and would learn to expect her to do it all without his input.

He went inside and greeted the dog, then jogged up the stairs to their master suite, his briefcase swinging from one hand. As she watched him go, she realised all of a sudden that the casserole dish had begun to burn the palm of her hand.

* * *

Bea sat at her dressing table in a light pink bathrobe, the blush brush in her hand. She dabbed it against one cheek, then the other. She wasn't one to wear much makeup and wondered what the expiration date on her blush might be. Better not to look, really. She'd probably be horrified by what she discovered.

She remembered fondly the first time their daughter, Danita, had tried out her blush. She'd found it on Bea's dressing table when she was only two years old. She'd dug into the blush until she'd loosened the entire thing and then plastered it over her sweet, chubby cheeks, the dressing table, the carpet and the walls. There were blush-coloured handprints on the white paint for days before Bea could finally scrub them clean, but she'd left one of the prints there.

She bent at the waist to look at it now. She'd hung a small frame around it and had an engraving added to the frame that stated the date, the medium (blush) and the artist (Danita Pike). They'd even painted around it when they'd updated the house a decade earlier, and again last year. The blush had faded until it was barely more than a smudge now, but it still held the distinctive shape of Dani's pudgy little hand. Bea's throat tightened at the sight, and she lovingly touched a finger to the frame.

Dani was so big now. It was hard to believe how much time had passed. To Bea, it felt like a moment ago. When the children were small, older ladies would tell her to cherish each moment since it would pass in the blink of an eye, and she'd wonder how that was possible since every day seemed to drag on forever. But they were right — the days were long but the years were short, and now both of her children had flown from the nest and were adults, navigating the big, wide world alone.

"What are you wearing?" Preston wandered out of the closet in his boxer shorts.

He was still buff after all these years. The ravages of child-bearing hadn't been his burden to bear, and he'd managed to continue attending a boot camp class three mornings per week for the past fifteen years, even during the time when Harry had decided to try out rowing as a school sport and required someone to drive him to practice every morning at five a.m.

"I bought that eggplant dress, the one with the swooping neckline. Don't you remember? I modelled it for you a few weeks ago."

He grunted. "Oh, right. What should I wear?"

"You told me not to get you anything, that you'd take care of it. Please tell me you've thought about your outfit. I've got a photographer coming. I wanted the photos to be special." Her voice grew louder. She could hear it happening and saw him shrink away. He hated it when she became what he called "emotional." She always had to monitor herself, pull back, keep things positive and quiet in case it caused Preston stress. It was exhausting sometimes dealing with his many idiosyncrasies. But even in the midst of all of it, she loved the man. She couldn't help it. They'd spent most of their lives together. More time together than apart.

"I forgot, sorry. But I can wear the navy suit."

"Not with my purple dress." She shook her head, then held still to apply her lipstick. "The black one will work."

"It's a bit tight."

"I know, but what can we do about it now?"

He sighed. "You know I hate it when I don't have something decent to wear. People will think I look ridiculous in that suit. It's ten years old and far too small for me."

"I don't know what to tell you," Bea replied. Really? He was going to blame this on her?

"'Sorry' would suffice."

"Sorry. Did you bring home that coffee machine I ordered? I had it sent to your office since I've been in and out of the house and didn't want to miss the delivery."

"Oh, I cancelled that order," he said matter-of-factly. "We don't need it. I don't even drink coffee."

"*I* do," she said, her brow furrowed. "You know how much I love it."

"Do you?" He acted as though he didn't hear her words but was responding by rote.

"Yes, I do. I've wanted an espresso machine in the house forever, and you've never let me get one."

"Seems wasteful," he replied, holding different ties up to his neck as he studied his reflection in the mirror. "Just drink instant."

Bea watched him, anger building in her chest. She pushed it down and stood to her feet. He had no problem buying himself an automatic golf doohickey that he spent hours putting balls at. Or the rowing machine he never used in the basement gym. Or countless other contraptions he'd sworn he needed and yet were currently gathering dust. She rarely asked for anything for herself.

Picking a fight with him right now over a coffee machine would be silly and pointless. They could talk about it tomorrow. They had guests arriving soon, and she needed him in a good mood so he would help entertain them rather than disappearing into the den with a glass of Scotch to brood over the latest football game.

One advantage of having spent over two decades together was that Bea had learned when to fight and when to pull back and realise something else was going on in her husband's mind. When he was anxious, he got snippy and combative, blaming her for every little thing even when he knew it wasn't her fault.

"Are you okay? What's going on? You're acting a little bit uptight, like you're anxious. Is it the party? Or did something happen at work?"

He sat on the bed, his shoulders sagging. "We might as well talk about it now rather than later, although I'd hoped to be dressed. Still, I might burst my jacket if we have this conversation while I'm wearing the black suit."

She ignored the jab and pulled her chair up to the bed, sat facing him, and took his hands in hers. She kissed his fingers, then squeezed his hands.

"What is it? Tell me what's on your mind."

Tears filled his eyes. "You know I love you."

"Of course I do." Her spine straightened.

"I can't do the vow renewal." His gaze met hers, his deep brown eyes full of sadness.

"Why not? We wrote new vows—they're not the traditional ones. It'll be fun." She didn't understand. Why was he backing out now after all their work on lighthearted, even teasing vows in which they promised to do things like always replace the toilet paper and never eat the last Tim Tam without asking the other person first? The vows were cute. Everyone there would love them. It made no sense to back out now.

"I've met someone else."

The words hit her like a slap to the face. "What do you mean, someone else?"

"Another woman. We're in love."

"No, you can't be... *We're* in love. You and me."

He sighed. "I'm sorry, Bea. I know this comes as a shock. It's something of a shock to me as well. I didn't see it coming. I didn't go looking for it, but here I am."

"This can't be happening." She pulled her hands free of

his and stood to pace the room. "We've got a hundred people coming to celebrate our marriage in less than an hour."

"I know it's bad timing, we can still have the party. No one else has to know. But I thought it would be in bad taste to renew our vows when... Well, you know."

She wrung her hands together. "How long has this been going on?"

His cheeks coloured. "Does that matter?"

"Yes, of course it does!" she shouted.

He cringed. "Don't get emotional."

"How dare you tell me not to get emotional? You're always saying that. But if this isn't the time to get emotional, I'd love you to please tell me when is!"

He shook his head and walked to the closet. "I can't talk to you when you get like this."

She followed him. "You have to talk to me, Preston. This time, you can't walk away and hope the conflict disappears. You have to face it. Tell me what it is you're trying to say."

"It's been going on for a year."

Beatrice's stomach roiled like she'd been sucker punched. She lurched backwards away from her husband. *No, no, no!*

"We love each other. She's been there for me when I went through a hard time at work. She understands me. We've made plans for the future."

Bea's eyes filled with tears. This couldn't be happening. They'd planned to travel once the children left home. They were going to enjoy their golden years together. After all their hard work, this was the time to enjoy each other's company. They'd had children together, they were a family. He couldn't build another life without them in it. How could he walk away?

"But what about *our* plans? Our family?" She stifled a sob.

"I want a divorce."

Two

THE PARTY itself was little more than a blur. Bea pushed herself to smile, to make idle chitchat, to serve drinks and plates of food to the guests who filled their home and spilled out onto the patio and into the backyard. She'd used twinkle lights to make the garden look like a starry wonderland.

From anyone else's perspective, the anniversary party was a huge success. The vow renewal was intended as a surprise for the guests, so they weren't aware it had been removed from the agenda. From her point of view, it was nothing more than a sham. Every congratulation she received was like a knife to her heart. Especially when Danita and Harry arrived. She wanted to cry at the happy looks on their faces as they hugged her and kissed her cheeks.

She'd have to tell them the marriage was over. That was the most difficult thing of all. They'd been so proud of her and Preston over the years — they'd recount the details of the divorces of their friends' parents and then say how grateful they were that they didn't have to go through that. *Their* parents wouldn't get a divorce. *They* were happily married. It was all Bea could do not to run to her room, throw herself down on the bed and scream into the plush pile of pillows.

Every now and then, she'd recall a past anniversary celebration — a happier time. The first anniversary, they hadn't been able to afford to do much so had stayed in a little cabin in the mountains. They'd spent every single moment with one another. They didn't need expensive accommodations or a long list of exciting things to do or places to see. Instead, they'd explored each other, talked until the wee hours, lounged in the small hot tub and laughed over the events of their first year together.

Twenty-five years later, the memories were faded like old photographs. And she was holding back tears as she waved goodbye to the last of their guests. She stood by the front door, bent at the waist and doing everything she could not to cry. There was still so much to clean up. Thankfully, the two wait staff she'd hired were already in the kitchen washing dishes. But the entire house looked as though a herd of elephants had passed through. She'd been up since dawn preparing for the party, and now she'd spend hours cleaning up.

She couldn't face it. It was too much.

Preston walked down the stairs carrying a small roller bag. He set it on the tiled floor and pulled it to the door. He'd changed out of his suit and into a pair of jeans with a red jumper. His hair was tousled, with touches of grey at the temples. He was fit and tanned, and his brown eyes were untroubled. Suddenly she felt a hundred years old, dowdy and fat. She'd never managed to lose those last ten kilos that she'd gained when she had Harry. It hadn't bothered her much before, since she'd been secure in her relationship. But now she was self-conscious.

"Where are you going?" she asked.

He stopped beside her, sighed. "I'm leaving. I think it's best I go now."

"But we've got to talk about this. It's so sudden."

He ran a hand over his hair. "Geri is coming to pick me up. My car needs some work done, I'll pick it up later in the week to take to the garage."

"Geri? Is that her name?"

He nodded. "We can talk more on the phone. I'm sorry this seems sudden to you, Bea. But for me, it's been coming on a long time. I'm only surprised you didn't realise that. You're always so in your own head."

The insult pierced her heart. He'd thrown the same words at her many times over the years, but in the past, it'd felt like a lighthearted jab. As though her ditziness was adorable in some way. But coupled with his rejection of her and their lives together, it was as though the words were a way to describe how she didn't measure up, how she wasn't enough for him.

"Don't leave, not yet." She begged him. The sound of her own voice made her squirm. This wasn't her. She was the confident, cheery wife who always made her husband smile and who never whined or used manipulation to get her way.

He glanced up at the sound of a car pulling around the driveway and stopping at the stairs. "I can't stay. It's over, Beatrice. There's nothing much more to talk about."

"We were going to travel," she offered weakly.

"I want to be with Geri. We're in love. We're building a life together. This life is over for me. Actually, it was over a long time ago. We've hardly spoken in years."

"That's not true." Her brows knitted together. "We speak all the time."

"Not about anything that matters," he countered.

And she couldn't argue with him on that. It was true — much of their conversation was about the kids, or the house, or his work, or her latest recipe. When had they stopped communicating like soul mates? Like two people who were deeply in love. Probably around the same time he started his affair.

And then he was gone. He didn't kiss her goodbye or call back over his shoulder with a smile and a twinkle in his eyes the way he usually did. He simply shut the door behind him and walked away, pulling his little wheelie bag behind him. It thunked down the stairs, and Bea watched through the glass strip beside the front door. Tears streamed down her cheeks— she didn't bother to hold them back.

How could her marriage be over so suddenly? Perhaps they weren't communicating or connecting the way they used to — but that's why marriage was described as work. You were supposed to put in the time and effort to reconnect and build that communication if it dipped. He wasn't doing the work. He was walking away with a newer, younger model.

The car parked in front of her house was a sporty red BMW. She vaguely recalled seeing a payment to a BMW dealership on a credit card statement months earlier. But Preston had waved off her questions with a story about a mistaken transaction that he'd deal with the next day. It'd seemed odd at the time, but she'd trusted him completely.

She didn't pay the credit card bill—he did. She always looked it over, though, so she could mark in the margin what each of her own personal expenses were so he could log them meticulously in the accounting software he used to track their finances. She'd never even logged onto the software before. He took care of all their finances, and she'd never had reason to question that.

She wiped her cheeks dry and went into the kitchen to pay the wait staff. Then she took a final glance around the house at the carnage the party had inflicted on her perfectly styled home and climbed the stairs for bed. The mess would still be there in the morning, and she didn't have even the slightest energy left to deal with anything more that night. Once in their bedroom, though, she found she couldn't face sleeping in the king-sized bed, and instead crashed on the couch in the living room.

* * *

The next morning, Bea woke on the couch. Her neck had a crick in it from having her head turned to one side for most of the night. When she looked in the mirror, there was a seam crease down one cheek from the couch cushion. And her heels were covered in blisters from the stilettos she'd worn during the party. She hadn't noticed the pain at the time, but now the blisters were excruciating, and one had burst in the night and felt raw.

As she splashed water on her face, she heard her mobile phone ring. She hurried to answer it and saw that it was Danita.

"Hi, honey," she said.

"Mum, I'm surprised you're up. I was going to leave you a voicemail."

"It's not early, is it?" Bea replied, squinting at her watch. She'd have to find her glasses so she could see what time it was but couldn't remember where on earth she'd left them in the craziness of the party the previous night.

"Yes, but I'm sure you were up late cleaning. I know you— there's no way you could've gone to bed in a mess. Did Dad crash as soon as the last guest walked out and leave you to do the clean-up all on your own, as usual?" Danita often criticised the way her father treated Bea. In the past, it'd warmed Bea's heart to know that her only daughter cared enough to notice the little things. But now it made her grimace.

Danita might make jabs about her dad, but she adored him. She'd always been Daddy's little girl, and even now she called him regularly to talk about whatever was going on in her life. He had plenty of time for his children now they were grown. They were his priority — it's what he always said, but in reality he'd prioritised work, or his own activities, over them for much of their childhood. It was a shame Bea hadn't been his priority in recent years like she was early in their marriage. Maybe things would've worked out differently.

"Actually, you'll be pleased to know I went right to bed and left everything for today. Thankfully, the waiters put the food away and washed the dishes before they left."

"Wow, Mum — I'm impressed. Maybe you're growing." Danita laughed.

"Or just getting old."

"That too. Hey, I want to talk to you about something. And I don't want you to get upset."

"Okay." This didn't sound promising. Whenever Danita had something she needed to discuss, it usually involved a large amount of money leaving Bea's bank account.

"You know I've been struggling with my social work degree. The more I study, the more I realise it isn't for me."

"Yes, but we talked about this. You should finish the degree and have the qualifications behind you before you look for something else to do. You need a degree, Dani."

Bea pulled on a pair of tracksuit pants and a jumper, then ran a brush through her hair, the phone on speaker beside her.

"I know that's what you suggested, but I don't feel right about it. Every semester costs a fortune, and I don't want to make you and Dad pay for something that I'm never going to use. I need some time to think about what I want to do with my life."

Bea took the phone off speaker and pressed it to her ear as she walked downstairs. "You let me and Dad worry about your tuition. I'm afraid if you take time off from study, you'll lose your momentum. It's really easy to get caught up in the busyness of life and forget or not have an opportunity to go back and finish your qualifications. You might meet someone, fall in love and have a baby, and then your career will go right out the window."

"That was your experience, Mum. It won't be mine. I'll get a degree, I promise. But I've already withdrawn from next semester."

Bea gasped. "What? Why would you do that without telling me?"

"I'm telling you now."

Bea slumped onto a stool at the breakfast bar in the kitchen. She suddenly felt sick to her stomach. Her husband had left her. Now Danita had dropped out of university. What else could go wrong? "What will you do? Because I can tell you right now, I'm not going to pay for you to swan around Sydney with your friends."

"I know that, Mum. I've already spoken to Pa about moving to Coral Island."

"What?" Her father rarely spoke to any of her family. She hadn't been to see him in three years. And now he was offering to house her grown child?

"He's got that cottage on the beach, the one you used to live in years ago. It's a bit rundown, but he said that if I renovate it, I can live there rent free for as long as I like. He's giving me a budget to work with and everything."

"You're going to move out to Coral Island, in the middle of nowhere, to live as a beach bum?" Bea's head throbbed, and she rubbed her temple with her fingers.

"It's not the middle of nowhere, Mum. You grew up there —you should know that. And yes, I'm going to be a beach bum for a while. There are worse things. Besides, I'll get a job and earn my keep. With free rent, that should be easy enough to manage. In the meantime, I'll renovate the cottage and think about what I want to do with my life. I might even be able to save up the money to travel to Europe before I go back to university."

"If you have to catch a ferry or a plane to get somewhere, it's the middle of nowhere. Trust me."

"You're not seeing the big picture, Mum."

Bea shook her head. This was too much. Her daughter had been top of her class at one of the most prestigious private schools in Sydney. Both Bea and Preston had been disappointed when Dani had decided to study social work, a degree that didn't have a high-level entry requirement, when she could've gotten into anything she chose. But they'd been proud that she wanted to do something to help those who needed it most.

Now she'd spend her days painting a rundown shack in a bikini. Bea had to talk to Preston — he'd convince Dani it was a bad idea. He had a talent for bringing people around to his way of thinking. But of course, there was the little issue of the divorce to contend with. Perhaps he wouldn't care what his daughter did now that he had a brand-new life with someone else.

"Fine. I can see you're not going to budge on this, and I have a splitting headache plus a house that looks as though it was part of some kind of global war. So, I'm going to let it go for now. But we'll talk about this again soon. Okay?"

Danita laughed. "Okay, Mum. Whatever you like. Although if you want to reach me before I leave, I'm taking the ferry to the island in three months. I've got to finish the current semester plus my job at the library and tie up some loose ends, pack my things on campus, and so on. I'm sure we'll see each other dozens of times before I go."

"Let's talk soon. I love you."

She hung up the phone, then leaned her forehead on the cool marble bench with a groan. At least Harry was still happily ensconced in his first semester at university. He was studying science with the intention of moving into medicine.

She clearly remembered the first time he'd said he wanted to be a doctor. She'd found him giving CPR to a dead magpie, dragged into the house by their cat, when he was five years old. He'd turned to her with that solemn look he got when he was doing something he cared about and told her he'd chosen his future career, even though the bird didn't make it.

She could cling to the fact that Harry was living up to his potential and not giving up everything they'd worked towards, like his sister, or tearing their family apart, like his father. She surveyed the damage. Then with her head held high, she got to work cleaning up the mess.

Three

THE NEXT FEW weeks passed quickly and in a haze of anguish, delirium and denial. Bea wandered between her engagements baking cakes for a function at the high school, volunteering at the local RSPCA and helping organise and run a fundraiser for the Rotary Youth Club to send several students on international exchange the following year.

She'd always been a joiner—had participated in civic programs for years. There was nothing she loved more than to give back to her community. Having grown up on Coral Island, where the lifestyle was centred around lazing on the beach and finding the best fishing spot, she'd embraced the city and its rapid pace.

But after Preston's announcement, she couldn't find the enthusiasm she needed to enjoy any of it. All she could think was that it was futile. None of it mattered. If the person who was supposed to love her most in the world could discard her at a moment's notice, why bother volunteering, or baking, or doing anything, really?

She pretended to be fine for the sake of the kids. Clearly Preston hadn't spoken to them, and she was avoiding telling them what he'd done. She knew they'd be angry with him, but deep down inside, some part of her worried they'd blame her as well. He was the fun one, the parent who always took them to eat junk food or see the movie she'd told them wasn't appropriate. She was the killjoy. That's how she imagined they described her, anyway.

She organised every aspect of their childhood, she made the meals, packed the lunchboxes, washed and ironed the uniforms and cleaned the house. She didn't have time for all the fun activities at the end of the day. She was still too busy vacuuming and folding laundry.

They'd side with him and blame her. She could hear it now. Partly because she couldn't help blaming herself. Even though she knew logically that made no sense. It took two people to keep the spark going in a relationship. Both of them had fallen short in that department over the years. Not without good reason, of course — life was difficult, busy and demanding. At the end of the day, neither one of them had much left — energy, affection, desire. But if the children sided with their father — the man who'd had an affair and left her to start his life over right when they were supposed to be enjoying the golden era after all that hard work — she wasn't sure her tender heart could take it.

One morning after she'd put on workout gear in order to exercise in the home gym, but instead ended up watching a rerun of *Ellen* slumped against the front of the treadmill while she ate giant handfuls of potato chips and cried over a child prodigy who played the violin so beautifully she was certain angels were singing, her phone rang.

She'd taken to screening calls, which wasn't at all like her. She was usually the life of the party, always ready for a conversation, happy to talk to anyone at any time of the day or night. Her friends knew that if they picked up the phone and told her they were having a bad day, she'd drop everything to bake them a chocolate gateau with cherry fondant and bring it right over to talk.

"Hello," she muttered around a mouthful of crisps.

"Bea, it's Preston. You sound strange. Are you okay?"

She swallowed and climbed off the treadmill. "I'm working out in the gym. What is it?"

"I need to talk to you about the house."

"What about the house?" She opened the back door so Fudge, her five-year-old pug, could go outside to pee.

"I'm going to sell it."

Her eyes widened. "You can't sell it. I live here."

"I know, and I feel terrible about that. But the problem is that I want to buy a new place in Melbourne."

"You mean for you and Geri?"

He cleared his throat. "Yes, that's right. And I need the equity from the Sydney house to make it happen. The market in Melbourne has really gotten out of control. You wouldn't believe how expensive houses are in certain suburbs."

Her cheeks burned. "I don't need a lesson in real estate, Preston. You can't sell this house because it belongs to both of us."

"Actually, it's in my name. The entire trust we used to purchase the house and our other real estate is in my name. Don't you remember? When we closed, you were busy with obstetrician appointments and baby Lamaze classes and all that stuff, so you told me to do all the paperwork myself."

"I didn't mean you should cut me out of decisions about the house completely! This is our house. We've lived here together for almost twenty years." She was livid. A flame of rage lit in her gut, and she followed Fudge out into the backyard to pace.

He coughed. "The fact is, I'm the executor of the trust, so I've got a real estate agent swinging by later. I'd appreciate it if you'd let them in to look around. They'll want to take photographs tomorrow and get the listing up by the weekend. You're still named as an equal beneficiary of the trust, so you'll get half the proceeds."

"How long do I have?"

"In this market, the agent thinks it will sell fast."

"So, what do you suggest I do for a place to live?"

He sighed. "That's really up to you, Bea. I can't take care of everything for you forever. You know that, right? I've done it for twenty-five years. Now it's time for you to stand on your own two feet."

He hung up before she could respond. She gaped at the phone, her face blazing. Did he really just tell her that she'd lived off him and let him do everything in their life for the entirety of their marriage? Him! The man who hadn't washed his own underwear once in over two decades and wouldn't be able to identify the toilet cleaning solution in a lineup if his life depended upon it?

Her head began to spin, and she lowered herself onto the porch swing with a squeak. She was about to be homeless. She had no idea how much money she had or how the trust worked. There were various friends over the years who'd warned her she shouldn't let Preston manage all the money without knowing what was going on with their affairs, but she'd waved them off with a laugh. He was her partner in life. They loved one another, and she trusted him completely. She had no need to keep her finger on the pulse of their finances.

Now she knew the truth. They'd been right all along.

* * *

The idea came to her one day when she was in the middle of grocery shopping. She'd filled her shopping cart with at least a dozen items before she realised that everything in the cart was for Preston. He liked the white saltines—she preferred wholemeal. But of course, she got the white for him because Preston got what Preston wanted. He liked steak—she preferred fish. Preston loved sponge cake—she hated it and would much rather have a nice packet of chocolate biscuits.

She put back all the groceries and started again with the things she liked to eat. The entire process had her eyes glistening with tears, but she refused to cry in the canned foods aisle.

Where would she live?

Preston was going to Melbourne as soon as the house sold. Harry was in the city at his dorm. And Dani was about to move out of her dorm and live on Coral Island in the small beach cottage where Bea had lived during her younger years. She missed that cottage and wondered how much it'd changed. It'd been years since she'd seen it. Her last visit to the cottage had been with her mother before she died.

The wallpaper had been peeling off the walls, the floors had holes in them, and the roof leaked. It was as though nature was reclaiming the patch of sand beyond the dunes where it sat. How could Dani go and live there in that remote and secluded location alone? She was certainly far more adventurous than Bea had ever been at that age.

All Bea had wanted was to get away from the island. It was beautiful and picturesque and full of people who knew everything about her and her family. It held so many painful memories of the mother she'd lost and the brother she no longer spoke to. The father she rarely saw. And yet now, with her heart aching over the loss of her husband and their family home, something inside her drew her back. She was homesick for the first time in over two decades.

That's when the realisation dawned — she should go to Coral Island with Danita. It was perfect. The cottage required far too much work for Dani to do alone. What experience did she have with housekeeping, let alone renovations? It was Bea who'd done all the work repairing, rebuilding and decorating their family home. She'd participated in every single aspect of the renovations on their house. Dani didn't know how to clean a toilet, let alone select and install one.

Besides that, Bea had nowhere to go. In a few weeks, she'd be homeless when Preston got his way. Instead of waiting for him to toss her out to live on the streets or to sleep in her car, or more likely the local motel, she could be proactive and head home to the island. The thought brought an enormous amount of peace to her soul.

Home. That's where she should go. And the idea of living with Dani again, however briefly, was more than appealing. She missed having her daughter around all the time. Of course, there was the small problem of Dani wanting this time alone as a kind of meditation that would allow her to choose a life path. But surely she wouldn't mind if Bea tagged along. She would make herself scarce. Dani would hardly know she was there. And she could offer up baked goods as a bribe if all else failed. Dani had always had a sweet tooth.

The only question was, what would Dad say?

* * *

The house sold within the first month of being listed. Preston was right yet again. But Bea no longer minded. She had a plan. She spent every waking moment preparing for the move. Preston had already come to pick out the pieces of furniture and other things around the house he wanted to keep. Then she packed up the rest and had removalists take what she didn't need to a storage facility. Anything that wasn't valuable or sentimental enough to keep, she sold on GumTree or gave away to the local thrift shop.

She still hadn't told anyone in her family what she was doing, and as far as she knew, Preston hadn't informed either child that they were getting a divorce and selling the house. It was as though both of them were engaged in a game of chicken, and so far, neither of them had called the other's bluff. The longer they went without saying anything, the more determined Bea was not to be the one to do it, although she knew it was immature and that in the end, the children deserved to know the truth.

So the weekend before her move, she contacted Harry and invited him to the house for dinner. Since everything was packed up, she ordered takeaway Chinese food and set it up in the den on the top of cardboard boxes.

Fudge trotted into and out of every room repeatedly. Ever since the movers came, the dog had been on edge. He'd run around looking for the couch, then make for his bed and leap into it with a look of distrust on his face as though he was certain she was about to snatch it out from under him.

When Harry came in, he gaped in astonishment.

"Hi, Mum. What's going on in here?" His brown curls hung to his collar, and his brown eyes were warm and full of surprise.

"Hey, honey." She kissed his cheek. "You look thin, and your hair is in dire need of a cut."

He rolled his eyes. "Yeah, that's really the pressing issue right now. Have you been robbed?"

Bea led him to the cardboard furniture. "Look, I ordered us some Chinese food. And we can sit on these boxes to eat."

"Mum..."

She sighed. "Take a seat and I'll tell you all about it."

He sat, his legs awkwardly crossed in a pair of oversized jeans. "Okay, I'm sitting."

She sat as well, then opened a box of food as she spoke. "You know that Dad and me have been having problems lately. Right?"

"I guess." He frowned.

"And sometimes people drift apart. They can love each other, but things get in the way of that."

"Mum, what's going on?"

She braced herself. "Your father and I have been struggling to connect for a while and something's happened that means we can't keep going the way have been. We're getting a divorce."

His nostrils flared. "I can't believe it. When did this happen? Why haven't you said anything before now? Surely you can work it out. Get some counselling or something."

Bea didn't want to string Harry along. Letting him believe there was hope, when there wasn't, would be cruel. She couldn't do it. "I was hoping Dad would talk to you about it."

"Why Dad?" Harry's cheeks were bright red, his eyes narrowed. "It's his fault, isn't it?"

Bea bit down on her lower lip to keep from crying. She had to stay strong in front of Harry. The last thing he needed was for her to be a blubbering mess.

"He's met someone else."

"No, he can't do that. That's not right." Harry's brow furrowed, dark and thunderous.

"I know it's difficult for you to understand, but it's true. He's met someone and they're in love."

"What?!" Harry's eyes glistened with tears. His mouth slammed shut.

Bea reached out a hand to squeeze his arm. "I'm sorry, honey. I know this is difficult to hear. But he'll always be your dad. He's simply starting a new chapter." She couldn't believe the words were coming out of her mouth. What she wanted to do was scream from the rafters that it wasn't fair, that he'd betrayed them all. But she couldn't do it. It would break Harry's heart. She could deal with her own pain, but she couldn't bear her son to be in anguish. He'd have enough to work through without her making things worse.

"He'll always be your father and he loves you very much, this is between him and me."

"Where will he live?" Harry asked, blinking back the tears.

"They're moving to Melbourne. Your Dad needs to sell the house so he can buy one for him and his fiancée down south."

She waited and watched for Harry's response. His eyes flashed. "He's selling our home?"

"I'm sorry, honey. I wish I didn't have to tell you any of this. But since your father seems to be avoiding the conversation, I decided that it was time to say something. He really should have told you himself."

Harry rubbed a hand over his mouth. "He said you were having problems about six months ago, but I thought you'd resolved all that since you had that big anniversary party and everything."

Anger flashed through her head like a bolt of lightning. "I wish he'd told *me* we were having problems. Great communication skills, huh?" She bit her lip. Her goal all along had been to avoid criticising Preston. He was Harry's father, and she didn't want their son to be any angrier with his dad than he had to be. "I'm sorry—I shouldn't have said that. He's your dad, and I know you love him."

"You love him too, right?"

"Of course I do."

"So, why can't the two of you work this out?"

"Did you hear me mention the girlfriend?"

He sighed. "Okay, yeah. I guess that makes it difficult. But I can't believe this is happening. I'm so angry with him right now."

"You should be angry—that's perfectly okay. But I know you'll come around and forgive him. In the meantime, I have nowhere to stay. So I'm going to live with Pa on the island for a while."

"Isn't that what Dani's doing?" Harry arched an eyebrow.

"Yes, she is. And I'd appreciate it if you didn't say anything to her about it. I'd like to be the one to tell her my plans."

"Fine," he said. "Apparently we're a family who keeps secrets, so why stop now?"

She shook her head. "Don't be like that. I'm not keeping anything from you or from her. I need to be sensitive to my timing with Dani—that's all. She's going through a lot right now."

"I figured," he replied. "She hasn't told me anything specific, but I can tell she's unhappy. I think it's a good idea for her to move to the island and get some perspective."

Bea pulled back to regard her son through new eyes. "When did you get to be so wise?"

He grinned, reaching for a box of noodles. "I've got an amazing mother who taught me everything I know."

Four

BEA HAD AVOIDED TALKING to her friends in Pennant Hills about her upcoming divorce and the sale of her house, but she had to face them at some point. The house had an enormous SOLD sticker pasted across a sign in the front yard. She was living on cardboard furniture. And recently she'd bowed out of every social and civic commitment she'd made.

She'd left the Parents and Teachers Association — it made sense, considering Harry hadn't been at the high school in months. But she'd been reluctant to let it go. So many of her friends were members, and she'd been part of the association in some shape or form for eight years. It was a portion of her life she'd enjoyed and didn't want to give up. But it was time.

The catering contracts she had in place, she'd sold to another local caterer who was happy for the business. Then there was her volunteer position taking care of rescue dogs at the RSPCA. She'd miss it there. She knew everyone so well and loved spending time grooming and walking the dogs, giving them the love they hadn't received when out in the world. But she couldn't keep the volunteering up from Coral Island, so she'd handed in her notice.

So many accounts to close and commitments to bow out of, but she'd finally come to the end of her busy preparations. Her last task was to meet her best friend for lunch to tell her what'd happened in her life since the anniversary party twelve weeks earlier.

She'd spent so much time with her family over the years, there were only a few women who were her companions at dinner parties, golf, at the gym. She volunteered at school with them, and attended church alongside them. They were her friends, but she hadn't called a single one of them to tell them what Preston had said, or what he'd done.

She missed the friends she'd had in high school on Coral Island. She'd left them all behind when she went away to university and hadn't kept up contact with them over the years. They'd always been there for her, but now she knew very little about them or their lives.

Another regret for her to bury alongside the many others that were rising to the surface of her mind as she considered what she'd sacrificed for Preston and his life goals. It turned out the sacrifices had all been in vain. If only she could have a second chance at life, she'd do so many things differently.

She recalled the time her school friends had helped her sneak out of the house so the four of them could attend a party her dad definitely wouldn't have approved of. She slept on the second floor, so they'd used a ladder from the tool shed, pushed it up to the side of the house, and climbed up to tap on her window. Penny had brought a dress from her mother's closet, Evie had carried lipstick and blush in a bumbag around her waist, and Taya had driven.

They hadn't stayed at the party long. It turned out to be something of a letdown with adult men drinking and smoking as they ogled the girls from across the room. Instead, they'd headed to the beach, where they'd all gone skinny dipping in the warm, dark ocean and had laughed and squealed in embarrassment when Taya hid all their clothes behind a rock and they'd had to search for them in the dark.

The beach was deserted, so they'd lain in their underwear on the sand looking up at the stars and swapping stories about their hopes and dreams for the future. It was right before her mother had died, when life still seemed so full of promise. Not long after that, everything had changed. Bea wondered where the memory had sprung from—she hadn't thought of that night in years. It was one of her favourite memories, but it'd been buried by the pain of loss that came soon after.

Her favourite casual restaurant, *Pinky's*, was the perfect place say goodbye. She'd met Annie every Friday during school terms for coffee for years now. Even though Annie wasn't exactly the type of women she'd ever have imagined she'd become friendly with, they were neighbours and had run into each other so many times over the years they'd simply fallen together, in a way. Besides, it was good to get out in the sunshine and fresh air at *Pinky's* and to talk over the various aspects of their lives.

The drive to the restaurant was picturesque. Sweeping greens with the occasional gum tree, and a hedgerow that lined the circular drive. Bea stopped at the valet parking and handed her car over to the attendant. Then she walked into the building, adjusting her blue silk scarf so it hung perfectly over her white-and-grey suit.

Annie was already there waiting for her. She'd ordered her a cosmopolitan and was halfway through her own when Bea hugged her and took a seat.

"It's about time we got together again," Annie said, raising her glass in a mock toast. "I feel like I haven't seen you for an age."

They took a drink. Then gave their lunch orders to the

waiter. Bea asked for pot roast. She hadn't done much cooking lately and was craving a homestyle meal.

They chatted about the weather and their gym attendance, family dramas and neighbourhood conflict.

Finally, Annie changed topic with a half smile on her face. "You've been very quiet, Bea. What's going on in your life?"

Bea cleared her throat. "I have something of an announcement."

"Oh?" Annie leaned forward in anticipation.

"Preston has asked for a divorce."

"No! That's terrible. What on earth happened? You celebrated your anniversary not long ago." Annie's eyes narrowed. "Was it someone else?"

Bea nodded. "I'm afraid so. He's in love, he says. He's moved out, and we've sold the house. I'm heading to the closing after lunch."

Annie gasped. "I knew he wasn't trustworthy. Something about his eyes."

Bea frowned. There was nothing wrong with Preston's eyes and Annie had always gotten on well with him.

"What are you going to do now? And where will you live?" Annie's eyes glistened, and she squeezed Bea's arm.

Bea patted her hand. "Thank you for your concern, but I'm going to be fine. I've decided to go home to Coral Island for a while."

Annie arched an eyebrow. "I vaguely remember you saying you would never move back to the island."

Bea shrugged. "Things have changed. Besides, that was a long time ago when I still had the kids living at home. Life on the island can be slow and boring for teenagers. Thankfully, I'm no longer a teen, so it will suit me just fine. At least, I hope it will."

"There's no way you'll be satisfied with island life after being a Sydney resident for so long," Annie declared with a shake of her head. "You'll miss the amazing restaurants, going to the theatre, the festivals and the clubs."

"Most of the time, I did those things with Preston. Now that he's gone, I can't imagine I'll be hitting the clubs very often." Bea chuckled.

"I'm going to miss you," Annie said, smoothing her grey bob behind her ears with a fingertip.

"I'll miss you too. And you're always welcome to visit." She'd miss a few things about her life in Sydney, like their family trips to the beach or shopping downtown with Dani. But it surprised her to realise that most of the activities and places she'd experienced throughout her life in the city were easier to let go than she'd thought they'd be.

She'd had enough of the fancy restaurants, clubs, traffic, trains, crowds, malls, committees and associations. It would be a welcome break to get away from it all. She needed some time to herself. A chance to rest. She'd always believed that she and Preston would take that chance together, but now she'd do it alone. And the prospect scared and excited her.

* * *

She caught a taxi to the solicitor's office after lunch because Annie had insisted on her going out with a bang and had pressured her into drinking three cocktails, her stomach was in knots and her head spinning. She wasn't ready to see Preston again, but they both had to be at the closing, so there was no getting out of it.

He was there when she arrived, standing in the lobby looking fit and tanned.

The sight tugged on Bea's heart. She shouldn't miss him, should she?

Their family was supposed to be his first priority. All those late nights working and trips to Melbourne, when she'd had to sacrifice doing the things she wanted to do so she could watch the kids, help with homework, get them fed and off to bed, he was having an affair instead. She'd never know for certain because since his admission, she didn't trust anything he said or did. Once trust was gone, it could never be fully recovered.

"Hi, Preston."

Preston greeted her stiffly.

"I suppose we should get started." Bea didn't know what to say.

Bea and Preston walked into the solicitor's office together. Her chest was tight, and she was having difficulty breathing. Perhaps she was having a stroke. More likely it was a panic attack, although she'd never had one before, so she couldn't be certain. Either way, they had to sign the closing documents so that if she passed out on the floor, at least the paperwork would be complete.

She stifled a giggle at her own tipsy gallows humour, wobbled across the office floor and sat opposite the solicitor.

"Let's get this house sold," said the solicitor, a large man with a bulging stomach and a balding pate. He brushed the remnants of hair over his bald patch and sat with a huff in his enormous leather chair, then pushed paperwork across the desk to each of them. "Sign these, then swap and sign again. Simple, really." He grinned.

With a nod, Bea took the stack of papers and the pen offered and set about signing them. They'd gotten a good price for the house, and her half would set her up with a nest egg for the future. It was enough money that she could buy a unit somewhere if she wished.

"Where are you moving to?" the solicitor asked, looking back and forth between the two of them.

"Melbourne," Preston replied abruptly without looking up.

Bea didn't respond. She'd barely had the strength to tell

Harry and her friends about the divorce. She certainly wasn't ready to tell a stranger. And besides, for some reason, she felt odd about telling Preston she was headed to Coral Island. He knew her history with the place better than anyone else, and he'd have plenty to say about the move. Right now, she didn't want his judgement or his advice. All she wanted was to sign the paperwork and get out of there. Being so close to him made her sweat.

The solicitor left them to it while he poured himself a cup of coffee in the next room.

"Are you okay?" Preston asked in a low voice. "With everything that's happening?"

Was he concerned? He hadn't seemed very worried when he walked out. "I'm fine, thank you."

"I'll contact you about the divorce settlement soon," he said. "We should get things rolling."

"Have plans, do you?"

"We want to get married, if that's what you're asking."

She swallowed down a retort, and her eyes filled with tears. "Congratulations."

He didn't reply.

"If you need to reach me, please send correspondence to our post office box. I'll forward it when I have a new address."

"Oh? Where are you going?"

"I haven't figured out all the bits and pieces yet," she said. "I'm still living at the house. I'll be heading home now to get the last of my things."

He grunted. "Don't live in your car, Bea. It's tacky."

"What do you care?"

He glared at her. "You know I care."

"Really? Because you certainly hide it well."

"Don't go there. Not today," he hissed with a glance out the open door as though looking for someone.

"Fine with me."

Their exchange had cemented her resolve not to tell him anything more about her plans. He didn't deserve to know, and she didn't want his negativity. She was excited and nervous about going back to the island after so long away. She wanted to guard that part of her heart carefully, since even the slightest dampening might make her change her mind.

They finished up with the paperwork, and Preston said a muffled goodbye and hurried away. She watched him go, gaping at the suddenness of his departure. He'd seemed desperate to get away from her and back to his real life with his new fiancée.

With a sigh, she slung her purse over her shoulder and wandered out to call a cab to take her back to *Pinky's* to pick up her car. She was suddenly very sober and ready to get back to the house for her last night there.

Five

THE FLIGHT to Proserpine in northern Queensland was a short one. Bea had only packed two bags, one she'd checked and one carried on, plus a laptop and purse. She had a scarf wrapped around her hair and wore oversized sunglasses. It made her feel as though she was going on some kind of romantic journey to find herself. And helped distract her from the fact that she was leaving her entire life behind and was about to surprise her adult daughter at the airport. She ate the small packet of pretzels the flight attendant brought her and sipped a cup of ginger ale in the hopes that it would help calm her stomach.

She anticipated the surprise would be a good one. She'd brought a box of chocolates with her as a peace offering. Dani loved chocolate. Even when she was a toddler, she'd managed to sniff out any Bea might have hidden around the house. Once, Bea found her in the pantry with both doors shut and a box of chocolates beneath her arm, brown encircling her mouth like a thick trail of lipstick. She'd startled when Bea flung open the pantry doors to look for a box of flour, and her lower lip had quivered until Bea burst out laughing. She

41

couldn't admonish her—Dani was so cute and vulnerable standing there, chocolate covered and repentant. Instead, she'd scooped her up into her arms and kissed her sticky sweet cheeks.

"You're such a sweet tooth," she said. And Dani had smiled then, revealing her brown-coated teeth. Bea had laughed again and blown a raspberry on her soft, pudgy tummy.

Bea's only hope was that she could manage the same reaction today — chocolates, kisses and a broad smile.

The plane was a small one with only two columns of seating. She was near the front and grimaced every time the aircraft lurched or bumped in the turbulence. Heart thumping, she clung to the armrest as the plane sailed onto the runway. She breathed a sigh of relief as it taxied to a parking space. As she walked across the tarmac and into the tiny airport, the change of temperature felt as though she'd stepped into an oven. She'd have to strip off several layers before she went much further or she'd pass out. She certainly wasn't in Sydney anymore.

She stood in the airport, removing her coat and scarf as she scanned her surroundings for any sign of her daughter. Dani had told her she was taking a flight that landed a little earlier than Bea's, but she should still be waiting for the shuttle bus that would take the passengers to the jetty in Airlie Beach where they'd catch the ferry across to the island.

Outside the airport, with her luggage rolling behind her and her laptop bag, carry-on, and purse hanging from her shoulders, Bea trudged along the footpath to join the line of people waiting for the shuttle bus. She spied Dani near the front of the line. Her blonde hair shone beneath the sun and she wore a cute little fedora tipped to one side, her head lowered to look at her phone screen.

Where are you?

Bea sent her a text, smiling slyly to herself.
She watched as Dani tapped out a response.

I made it to Proserpine, waiting for the bus.

I wish I could join you.

Don't worry, Mum. I'll see you soon enough.

Maybe sooner than later???

Definitely.

Bea gritted her teeth. Surely her daughter wouldn't be angry with her for coming all this way. Besides, she still hadn't had a chance to talk to her about the divorce. At first, she'd waited for Preston to do it, and then she hadn't wanted to interrupt her daughter's frenzied preparations for life on the island. Now she had a sinking feeling she should've made the effort and gotten the conversation out of the way. How would Dani react to it all? She could be a tad dramatic at times. Didn't much like change.

She'd been diagnosed with autism around the age of ten. It was unusual for girls to be diagnosed at all, since they were so good at hiding it most of the time. But Dani's strong emotions had led them through several counsellors until one had suggested that a psychologist might be able to give them a diagnosis that would help. And it had. They'd found professionals who could give Dani the tools she needed to manage most things in her day-to-day life, but big changes and big emotions were still a challenge. Bea was amazed at how well her daughter had coped with quitting university and packing up to move to Coral Island.

The bus pulled into the parking lot and steered towards the front of the line. There was no time like the present.

Turn around.

Dani stared at the screen, then spun on her heel and locked eyes with Bea. Her sunglasses hid her response, and her mouth opened slightly. She pushed her phone into her pocket and beckoned Bea over. Bea apologised profusely to everyone in the line she passed until she stood in front of Dani.

"Surprise!"

Dani shook her head. "Mum, what are you doing here?"

She hugged Bea, then stepped back.

"Let's talk on the bus." Bea waved at the line ahead of them, and Dani saw it was moving.

The two of them walked slowly to the bus, giving the driver their luggage to store beneath the vehicle before they stepped inside. Dani found two empty seats and sat by the window. Bea slid in next to her.

"Please tell me what's going on," Dani said.

Bea turned to face her. "There's a lot to digest. So, I'm going to start at the beginning."

The bus lurched forward and pulled out onto the road. A sign pointed in the direction of Airlie Beach. The landscape was vividly green, with luscious vegetation and tall grass. The airport was surrounded by fields and seemed to have been dropped into the middle of nowhere. Brown and white cattle grazed nearby. The bus growled down the road, bumping over a pothole.

Bea held on to the seat in front of her. "Your father and I have grown apart. We've been fighting a lot."

"Really?"

"Since you moved out, things have gotten a lot worse."

She shook her head. "I'm sorry, Mum."

"Thank you, sweetheart."

"I'm sure you'll be able to patch things up though. You love each other."

Bea swallowed. "Yes, we do love each other. But there's a bit more to it now, I'm afraid. Your Dad met someone else."

Dani's eyes widened. "Does he love her?"

"It seems so. He wants a divorce."

"Why? I don't understand."

"I wanted him to tell you all of this himself. It's really inappropriate for him to leave it to me. But as usual..." Bea raised her free hand and shook her head.

Dani's eyes filled with tears and a single tear escaped down her cheek. "Why would he do this? We're a family."

"We're still a family, sweetheart." Bea looped an arm around Dani's shoulders and pulled her close. "This doesn't change that fact. But unfortunately, Dad and his new fiancée want to buy a house in Melbourne, so we had to sell our home."

"You sold the house?" Dani's cheeks turned red. "I didn't even get to say goodbye, Mum. That's not cool. It was my home too."

"I kept all your things. They're in storage."

Dani crossed her arms and faced out the window. "I can't believe you didn't tell me."

"I'm sorry, but I was going through quite a bit myself. It was hard for me to take one step at a time, let alone think about how everyone else would feel about what was happening."

Dani stared out the window for a long time, tears wetting her cheeks. She wiped them fiercely with the back of her hand, then straightened. "It's not fair, Mum. I wish you or Dad had said something before now. I can't believe you've done all this without talking to me."

"I'm sorry, sweetheart. You're right — we should've said something sooner. But you don't live at home any longer, you're an adult now. Sometimes Dad and me will do things without talking to you about it."

Dani's nostrils flared. "Yes, take a holiday without telling me, or redecorate the living room... but don't break our family apart and change your entire life without saying anything."

Bea sighed. "Please try to understand. This has been a hard time for us all."

Dani loosened her arms and met her mother's gaze. "You're right. I'm sorry, Mum. How are you feeling about it?"

"Blindsided, heartbroken, scared..." Bea swallowed around a lump in her throat. "That's why I'm here. I decided to come to Coral Island with you. We can both live in the cottage, and I can help you renovate. Let's face it, I'm the queen of renovation."

Dani laughed through her tears. "That is true. I could do with your help. I've been pretty stressed about how I would manage any of it. But I'm still angry at both of you."

"I can live with that. I'm basically homeless, and I need some time to recover, let my heart heal, figure out my next move."

Dani leaned into Bea and rested her head on Bea's shoulder. "I'm glad you came, Mum. And now I won't starve to death."

* * *

The ferry to the island was huge. Cars filled the bottom of the boat in long lines. Bea and Dani climbed the staircase to the top level and found a chair in the café. They each ordered a cappuccino, then sat by one of the many windows to watch the scenery passing them by. Within minutes, they were out at sea.

The ocean was a brilliant blue that Bea hadn't seen anywhere else in the world. The unique sediment of the region coupled with the purity of the water gave it an impossibly perfect hue. The sand that showed up in small drifts around the shoreline and on the banks of the islands that rose up alongside the boat was almost pure white. A pod of dolphins dove and splashed beneath their window. The July day was mild and sunny with a crystal blue sky.

"This is amazing," Dani said, sipping her coffee. "Why haven't we come here more often?"

Bea knew the topic would come up, but wasn't sure how to address it. "It was hard after my mother died."

"Is that why you never talk about Coral Island?"

"I suppose so." It was too much too fast. She'd already shared so much with Dani that day—she couldn't face the prospect of diving into her entire family history. Her head throbbed, and she felt as though she'd cried for hours, even though she'd barely shed a tear. She was tired, dehydrated and starving. Deep conversations would have to wait.

"What's Pa like?"

"Don't you remember?" Bea squinted against the afternoon sunshine as it slanted through the window.

"Yeah, of course I remember. But I haven't seen him much in years, and when I was little, all I saw was a man who was quiet and kept to himself. He took me fishing a lot. That's about all I can recall."

"And snorkelling."

"Yes, I loved snorkelling on the reef. The beautiful coral, the parrotfish that swarmed around us and nibbled at my toes. Those were some of my favourite times as a kid."

Bea smiled. "Mine too. I'm looking forward to doing those things again now that you're older."

The boat ride took over an hour. In that time, they stopped at two different islands for passengers to disembark. Finally, the ferry pulled up to Coral Island as the sun sank below the horizon. Dark shadows drifted over the ocean and finally brought a refreshing cool breeze that lifted Bea's hair from the back of her neck as she descended the stairs, one hand firmly on the rail.

It was hard to see much of the island with the sunlight gone. The streetlights were dim. All of the shops were closed, and the streets were almost bare. A small bus growled by to pick up the few tourists and locals who were left on the ferry.

Bea led Dani to the side of the ferry, where they collected their luggage. Then they stepped onto the dock, and she crossed her arms as she scanned the faces of those waiting to meet passengers.

Her father stepped forward, his grey hair lifting slightly in the breeze. He waved a hand, and she hurried to him, falling into his embrace with a sigh. "Dad, it's so good to see you." A lump rose unbidden to her throat. She swallowed it down. There'd be time to cry later. Her father had never been good with displays of emotion.

"You made it, then," he said, giving Dani a quick hug. "Good to see you both. You must be tired."

He picked up the handles for each of their wheelie bags and pulled them behind him. "Come on—let's get to the truck. We can talk on the way."

They followed him and climbed into his truck. Three across the front seat. It was cosy. Bea had to sit with her legs straddling the gear stick like she had when she was young. Nothing changed on the island, least of all her father, although he'd aged a lot since she last saw him. Was thinner and had more grey in his hair and the stubble on his chin.

"Thanks for meeting us, Dad."

He cranked the truck and put it into first. "I don't get many visitors."

She felt convicted by his words. "Time flies, I suppose."

"It sure does." He smiled. "No need for apologies. We can make up for lost time."

"Did you know Mum was coming too, Pa?" Dani asked.

"She called me a few days ago."

"Glad she let someone know," Dani murmured, looking out the window.

"Sorry?"

"Nothing."

"I've grilled some fish on the BBQ, if you're hungry."

"Starved," Bea replied. "That sounds delicious."

"Went spearfishing this morning. Caught a big old snapper."

"You're still doing that?" Bea had always worried about him spearfishing, especially with the number of sharks in the water around the Coral Island coastline.

"Best place in the world is under the water with a spear in your hand and nothing but your wits to save you." He chuckled. "Besides, it keeps me fed."

They drove along the coast road around the headland and then climbed one of the few hills on the island. The truck growled to a stop in front of a tall timber structure. Her father had built the house with his own hands. It sat on the point overlooking a towering cliff that led down to a cosy private beach, surrounded by black rocks where it met the azure waters. When she climbed out of the truck, a cool wind whistled through the scrubby trees that flanked the house.

She hugged herself while she waited for her father to unload the luggage from the back. The trees around the house had grown. The timber was more weathered. There was some kind of shed further along the driveway that hadn't been there before. But otherwise, the place looked exactly the same as it had throughout her childhood.

It'd been her mother's dream to build this house on the headland. They'd purchased the land when Bea was born. It'd taken her father ten years to build the place, along with running the hardware shop and providing for the family.

"The place hasn't changed much."

Dad grunted. "Nope."

"It looks good, Dad."

"Come on inside, then. Get out of this wind. We can put a fire on if you like."

Only Dad would think it was cold enough for a fire on a mild winter's evening on a tropical island, Bea thought with a wan smile.

With one last look around, Bea followed her father and Dani inside. Her heart thudded against her rib cage at the prospect of facing all the old haunts, the memories, the pain. She wondered for a moment how many of her old friends lived on the island. There'd been a few still around the last time she'd visited three years earlier, but she hadn't stayed long enough to catch up with any of them.

Preston hadn't wanted to be in her father's house for too long, and they'd finished up their holiday in a resort in Airlie Beach instead of on the island. She regretted that now. Too much pandering to her husband and not enough time with her own family. She wouldn't make the same mistake again.

* * *

After a delicious meal of fresh grilled snapper and vegetables from the garden, Dani and Bea unpacked and then Bea slumped down on the couch. Dad sat in his armchair, flicking through channels on the widescreen television fixed to the wall beside the fireplace in the living room. A small fire crackled in the hearth.

"Anything on?" she asked.

Dad grunted. "There never is."

"What do you usually do at night?"

He turned the television off and set the remote down on his armrest. "I usually watch something, read, go to bed. Sometimes I go down to the local pub with the boys. It's quiet at night on the island."

"That hasn't changed."

"Nope," he agreed. "I've been night fishing lately. And in summer I went spearfishing in the dark. It was a little more exciting than I like it."

"What happened?" Bea asked, her brow furrowed.

"A pretty big fish jumped in my boat because I left the torch on. And I had a close encounter with a shark."

"Dad!" she objected. "You shouldn't be spearfishing at night. That's so dangerous!"

He grunted. "I'm fine, tweaked my back a little but I'm managing. I decided I preferred to spearfish during the day after that anyway. Although, it's peaceful at night. The stars look nice too."

She sighed. "I can't argue with that. But what if something had happened to you? No one would've known."

He shrugged. "How is that different to any other time?"

"I'm sorry I haven't visited much." Guilt washed over her. She hated that she'd left him alone for so long. She'd convinced herself that she wasn't needed on the island. He was independent and happy with his own company. But she could see now that he'd been lonely, even with the friendships he'd maintained over decades. There was no substitute for family. And she hadn't been there for him when he needed her.

His grey hair was thick and wavy, his bright blue eyes full of life. But he was growing older, and she'd missed spending time with him for too many years. Who knew how much longer she'd have him, and she'd squandered that time pandering to the needs of a husband who didn't appreciate her.

"You've been busy. And Bradford's a big help."

She frowned. Her brother had never been the responsible one. That'd always been her role. When they were teens, she was the one who made sure Brad had food to eat, that he'd brushed his teeth and his lunch was packed. Dad was busy working and Mum was gone, so she'd taken on the role of parent. But Brad had acted out, and she'd been so frustrated with his lack of concern about their family.

"Really? Brad's been here?"

Dad walked into the kitchen and switched on the jug to boil. Bea followed him, her lips pulled into a tight line.

"He checks in, helps when I need it, that sort of thing. He's been the only one here for Christmas the past few years."

"I asked you to come to Sydney," Bea protested. It'd been no end of frustration for her that her father refused to travel. She'd had things to do in the city. It was the busiest time of the year for her and the kids—it made no sense for them to head to the island.

"You know I don't like to fly. And it's too far to drive. No, Brad and me—we had a nice time together. He even cooked."

"He cooked?" She quirked an eyebrow. Apparently, there were many things she didn't know about her baby brother these days.

"He's getting pretty good at it, too. Made an apple-infused pork roast last year."

Her eyes widened. "Wonders never cease."

"You should give him a chance. He's changed."

"That would be a miracle," she scoffed.

"I don't understand your attitude," said Dad as he poured hot water over a tea bag into a mug. "Tea?"

She shook her head. "No, thanks. My attitude is based on years of experience."

"That was a long time ago."

"Seems like yesterday," she huffed.

"Well, it wasn't. Time's passed—things have changed. And it's time you realised that. Welcome home, Sugar Pie." He dipped his head, picked up his cup, and walked out.

Six

THE NEXT MORNING, Bea rose early and looked at her phone. The pet-moving company she'd hired intended to deliver Fudge to the house later that afternoon. With a yawn, she changed into running gear and headed out before her father and Dani woke.

The morning was cold and yet beautiful in a way she'd forgotten the island could be. The wind had died down overnight, and everything was still. The sky was a deep blue. There was dew on the grass. Birds chattered and dived, catching the first insects in the early dawn.

The house perched happy and peaceful like a sentinel on the hill. She wandered around to the other side of the structure and located the pathway she recognised like an old friend. It meandered down the cliff in a lazy way and she followed it easily, hoping her knees wouldn't give her any trouble on the bigger vertical steps.

Overhead, a seagull squawked and circled, moving out on the air current to hover above the surging ocean. The sun sparkled on the peaks of water as though dancing across its surface. Waves curled to shore in a steady rhythm of sighing and shushing.

Bea ran the last few steps onto the sand. It was cold and damp underfoot, and she shivered and wrapped her arms around herself. She wore shorts and an oversized knitted jumper, and the cold travelled right through it. But the sun had already risen and would soon warm the sheltered sand. The cove was a small half-moon of beach with imposing cliffs surrounding it like a giant ice cream scoop had been there long ago. The sand lay in solemn shadow while the water was inviting.

She jogged towards the waves and dipped in her toes. It was warm and comforting. She sighed and raised her arms over her head, enjoying the feel of the sun on her face. This was exactly what she needed. It was good to get out of the city.

One end of the cove was blocked by black rocks. The other end had a thin wedge of sand around the outside of the rocks. The waves lapped the sand, but the water was shallow enough to walk through between sets. The long beach that stretched out into the distance on the other side of the rocks was already warm. Her feet revelled in the soft, dry sand. She filled her lungs with sweet fresh air. In the distance, she saw the outline of another of the Whitsunday Islands, its forested edges meeting the water like an emerald gown.

There was only one other person on the beach. A tall man threw a stick for a dog, who bounded into the waves to bring it back. She strode in that direction, watching in delight as the dog clambered from the waves and shook its long golden fur, soaking the man in the process. He shouted and ducked, but it was no use. Then with a laugh, he picked up the stick that'd been dropped at his feet and sent it sailing into the water again.

She marched by him, her gaze set firmly on the horizon. How far should she walk? There was no pressing need to be back at any particular time other than the fact that it was her first morning with her father. Even though they'd talked through dinner the night before, she wanted to spend more time with him.

"Good morning," she said to the man on the beach, with a nod of her head.

He was handsome. Muscular beneath a long-sleeved shirt. His legs were tanned under his board shorts. And he wore a cap pulled low over his eyes. He seemed young, but perhaps that was because everyone looked young to her these days. Sometimes she felt as old as Methuselah. And at other times, she forgot she was no longer twenty and tried to do something like jump on the old trampoline in their backyard — a move she'd instantly regretted when her internal organs seemed to shift positions with each bounce.

"Bumble Bea?" The man's voice shocked her out of her reverie and brought her back to the present.

She turned and looked at him with curiosity. There was only one person in the entire world who'd ever called her that name. But she hadn't heard it in decades. "Yes?"

He took off his sunglasses and sent her that wide, white smile she knew so well. It made her heart lurch the way it had since she was ten years old and he'd grinned at her on the school playground.

"Aidan Whitlock, I wasn't expecting to see you here." She laughed and went to give him a hug. Something deep down inside her broke open, and she wanted to cry with delight. It'd been so long, too long, since she'd seen her childhood sweetheart.

He stepped back and gazed into her eyes. His were blue and green with flecks of yellow. They crinkled at the edges. "Ditto. How long has it been?"

"I don't know. Let's see... I saw you after I finished university at that one party."

"But then you moved back to Sydney and out of my life forever." He pressed a hand to his heart in mock tribute.

She playfully slapped him. "You mean you moved to Brisbane to become a professional football player."

He shrugged. "That too. How are you?"

"I'm good. Actually, no, that's not true. I'm so used to saying that, I forget that there are other possible answers. I'm surviving at the moment. That's far more truthful."

"I'm sorry to hear that." His brow furrowed.

She waved a hand. "Don't be—it's fine. Well, it's not, but it will be. I'm going through some things, but I'll manage. How about you? What are you doing here? Taking a break from fame and fortune?"

He chuckled. "Didn't you hear I retired?"

"I don't really follow professional football. I watched a few of your games, though. Even though you played for the enemy, I barracked for you every time. Quietly, so my friends and family didn't disown me."

"Glad to hear it," he said. "But I left the sport five years ago. Forty is pushing it to be a pro athlete in any sport, let alone Rugby League. I had a few injuries one after the other and decided to call it a day. I moved back to Coral Island after my wife died, and now I work as the PE teacher at the primary school."

An image of the school flashed across Bea's mind. She remembered it clearly, as though it'd been only recently that she'd attended there with her long blonde pigtails and her button nose. It was where she and Aidan first met. They were in the same year four class, with Miss Plimpton. He'd helped her up when she fell and grazed her knees, then took her to see the school nurse.

It was corny to think about it now, but at the time, it'd been love at first sight. The two of them were friends until year ten when he finally asked her out. They dated for two years, only parting ways when he was recruited to the Brisbane Brumbies and she was accepted into Macquarie University to study business. She hadn't lasted long, withdrawing after her first semester to enrol in culinary school instead.

Perhaps Dani was more like her than she'd realised.

"You had an amazing career. Not many people last that long. But I'm sorry to hear about your wife."

"Thank you."

"I didn't know. I wish I'd realised. I would've sent you something. That must've been hard on you."

He nodded. "It was. We never had children—she got sick too young. She spent years fighting for her life. I thought everyone in Australia knew what'd happened."

"I don't read magazines or watch the news. I haven't since Dani was born. At first, it was because I was too busy, and then it was because I didn't want the kids seeing it, then I never went back to it because I didn't want the drama or anxiety."

"That makes sense. I'll have to try it myself. So much negativity in the media these days. Anyway, she died of breast cancer, and after she passed, I had to get out of there and go somewhere else." He threw for the dog again, a beautiful Golden Retriever who couldn't take his eyes off the stick and had no time for Bea. The dog launched into the ocean, sending salt water spraying in every direction. "I missed the island, and I saw there was an opening for a PE teacher. The principal let me start while I was studying part-time for my qualifications, since she knew me. And I'm still there three years later."

"Wow. Well, good for you — changing careers, overcoming grief, moving... You've navigated a lot."

She pushed her hands into the pockets of her shorts and kicked at the sand with one toe. The silence between them was awkward, full of all the things they hadn't said, all the goodbyes that were never quite right. He'd left before they had a chance to work out their future together. Their relationship had ended by default, with no closure. She'd been heartbroken at the time, but it was before email and social media. There'd been no way to get in touch with him. He'd left her behind, and she'd never quite recovered from it. But so much time had passed now that it was meaningless to say anything.

"I suppose I should get back," she said instead of the words that were piling up at the back of her throat. "Dad and Dani will be waiting for me."

"I see your father around town sometimes."

"Really? He never mentioned you were back."

"Probably doesn't want you to know," Aidan replied with a wink. "I'm the bad boy, remember?"

She laughed, her cheeks flushing. Her father had never liked Aidan. Thought he would break her heart. Turned out he was right about that.

"Not a bad boy exactly. Only bad for me."

"I guess the old guy was smarter than we realised."

Bea squinted to look more closely at Aidan's face and found him watching her with curiosity and warmth in his eyes. She looked away. "I guess so."

"And Dani is your daughter?"

"That's right. She turned twenty this year, if you can believe it."

He gaped. "Wow. That went quickly."

"It sure did. I have a son as well. Harry is eighteen."

"You've been busy, then."

"Very busy. I suppose I'll see you around the place," she said, stepping away in the direction of the cove.

"You're staying on the island?" He tented a hand over his eyes to watch her leave.

"For a while. Where are you living?"

"In the unit behind Mum and Dad's house. Do you remember it?"

She could picture it vividly. An impression of the two of them entwined on a couch sprang into her thoughts, and she blushed. "Oh, yeah. That place was great. So close to the beach."

"I like it," he said. "I'm building a house at Point Prospect. I move in next week."

"It's so beautiful there. I haven't seen it in years, but from what I recall, it's very picturesque."

"The community has grown a little, but still nice and quiet. Anyway, I'll see you about town, then. Glad we ran into each other."

"Me too." She waved and then turned towards home.

She still couldn't quite believe she'd come across Aidan Whitlock on the beach. She hadn't even run a comb through her hair yet, and no doubt had morning breath. He looked like he'd stepped out of a sports magazine, with his perfectly mussed sun-bleached locks and his athletic physique.

He'd moved back to the island. That was a piece of news Dad could've shared with her. Not that it would've impacted her life in any way, but it would've been nice to know that the man who broke her heart twenty-seven years ago was back and working at the school where they'd met.

She risked one last glance back at him and found him still watching her, his dog standing close by, dripping sea water onto the sand. With a pounding heart, she ducked her head and broke into a run around the rocks and across the cove.

Seven

WHEN SHE GOT BACK to the house, her father had already mixed up a batch of pancakes and was frying them on a griddle on the gas stovetop. Dani sat at the enormous split timber table in the dining room, the tall, double-story windows overlooking the view behind her, as she told her grandfather all about her life. He listened and nodded, occasionally grunting in response. Dani seemed to have warmed to him instantly and was confiding in him more than she had anyone other than Bea.

"So, I realised social work wasn't for me after all. And now I don't know what to do with myself. I don't want to waste money and effort studying something I hate."

"Makes sense," he replied.

"I'm sorry I didn't tell you all of this on the phone."

"Fine with me."

"I was feeling a bit fragile over the whole thing."

He grunted.

"You're feeling better, then?" Bea asked as she wiped her sandy feet at the door.

"Good morning, Sugar Pie," Dad said as he flipped a pancake. "Nice walk?"

"Lovely walk. It's so beautiful down at the beach this time of morning."

"I wondered where you were," Dani said. "Until Pa told me you'd probably gone walking. He said you always loved walks on the beach. Used to do it all the time when you were a teenager. Is that right?"

"I've spent many an hour on that sand. It helps me clear my head, think things through."

"I don't think I've ever seen you take a beach walk alone," Dani said.

Bea hesitated before responding. "I prioritised your father for a long time and he doesn't like walking on the beach in the morning — says the sand is too cold. He liked to have breakfast together instead."

"You should do what makes you happy."

"I'm beginning to come around to that way of thinking," Bea replied, kissing Dani on top of her head. "That looks delicious, Dad. I'll wash my hands and help you."

They finished making the pancakes together while Dani set the table. Then they sat on the bench seating around the table and ate. The pancakes were hot and fluffy. Coated with lemon juice, cinnamon and sugar, just like she'd eaten as a child, they made her nostalgic, and her tastebuds tingled.

She couldn't stop thinking about running into Aidan. He'd taken her by surprise. Aidan Whitlock was the last person she'd expected to see there. She hadn't kept up with the celebrity gossip over the years or she might've known more about his life.

There was a time when he was regularly on the cover of magazines or splashed across the socials, a media darling as the hottest new football player in the league. But it'd been too hard for Bea to see his smiling face and lithe form as the media discussed romances, achievements and every aspect of his life in painstaking detail.

She'd learned to avoid looking at the magazine racks when she went to the grocery store, and ignored the news. And then when the children were born she had no time for magazines or gossip. If she'd kept up with the news, maybe she would've heard about his wife and realised she might run into him on the island.

A memory drifted across her thoughts. Aidan holding her hand in the dark on that very same beach. The feel of his lips on hers, then his fingers winding through her long hair. Heat rushed up her spine.

"I saw Aidan Whitlock on the beach," Bea said suddenly.

Her father arched an eyebrow. "Oh?"

"He says he moved back to the island three years ago. Why didn't you tell me?"

Dad chewed a piece of pancake slowly, then spoke. "I didn't think it mattered."

"I suppose not." Of course it didn't matter. She was an adult woman, she'd moved on, gotten married, had children. Her broken heart had mended. Why would he tell her about an old boyfriend moving home?

"I was wrong about him, though," Dad said, surprising her. "He turned out to be a good man. I guess you can't always judge a man by the way he acts as a youngster. People change."

"That's big of you to admit, Dad. He was always a good guy, but he liked a prank or two."

"That he did." Dad's eyes sparkled. "But when I saw the way he nursed his wife all those years... Well, that kind of thing shows a person's true character." He cleared his throat and stared at his plate.

Bea knew what he was thinking. He'd had his own test of character taking care of their mother. He'd known the pain of loss. No doubt he realised that he and Aidan shared some things in common. She hated thinking about what Aidan must've gone through. The pain he'd suffered would've been difficult to bear.

"He must've struggled." She took a bite of pancake; the lemon was extra tangy. No doubt Dad had picked the fruit from the trees in his backyard.

"It was probably featured more in Queensland since he's from the Brumbies, but she was sick for a long time, from what I saw on the news. Very sad that she didn't make it."

"No kids, either," she added.

He sighed. "The best part of life."

"Really, Dad? You don't regret it, even after my teen years?" She laughed.

"Well, maybe... Just kidding. Of course I don't regret it. You and your brother were my biggest achievements."

His words warmed her soul and made her feel emotional. "I haven't seen him in three years."

"I know," Dad said. "He'll be excited to hear you're around again. He misses you. We both do."

Her throat tightened. As much as she wanted it to be true, she knew it wasn't. Dad was trying his best to smooth things over, but she and Bradford hadn't parted on good terms. They'd been so close once, but after Mum died, they'd had a falling out.

No matter what had happened between them, she shouldn't have let it go this long without seeing him and at least trying to talk things through. She'd neglected the people who loved her most. All because it was too hard, too far away, too many memories to contend with. Those were only excuses, though. She should make time for the people she loved.

"I thought I'd take you and Dani to see the cottage after breakfast."

"Oh, yes. Let's do that," Dani said, eyes sparkling.

"It's in bad shape. You won't be able to stay there right away—too much damage. But it's close enough that you can ride a bike or walk down there when you need to, if you're still keen on refurbishing the place."

"We're looking forward to it," Bea replied.

"Definitely. I can't wait. This is going to be so much fun." Dani clapped her hands together.

Dad chuckled. "Fun. Sure, that's one way of looking at it."

They finished up breakfast. Bea washed the dishes while Dani showered. Then they both dressed in old clothing and tugged on the gumboots outside the back door. Bea showed Dani how to turn the boots over and tap them out in case anything had crawled inside overnight. A gigantic spider landed on the porch.

Bea shivered and made a gagging sound. Dani danced in place, squealing. They both watched it scurry away, disappearing between the timber slats. "I forgot how many of those there are around here."

"Oh, disgusting. That thing was huge." Dani wiped her hands up and down her arms. "Is there anything on me? I feel like there's web on my jumper."

Bea laughed. "There's nothing on you. You're fine. Come on—get your boots and let's go. How did I raise such a city slicker?"

"You hate spiders too!" Dani objected.

"I have good reason. They have a vendetta against me. *You've* got nothing to worry about. You're not on their hit list."

Dani rolled her eyes. "That's silly, Mum. Besides, if it were true, what's to say they don't come after me in the same way? We are related, after all. Maybe spiders can sense that."

Bea huffed. "Now you're being ridiculous."

The drive down to the cottage was along a winding dirt track. It was overgrown, but Dad's truck traversed it easily enough. It didn't take long. Only ten minutes crawling along at a snail's pace. Dad pulled the truck up beside a tiny rundown cottage. The front porch looked out over a stunning blond beach between a pair of pandanus trees.

"Wow, look at this place. I haven't seen it in years, but it's even more beautiful than I remembered," Dani said, climbing out of the truck and running onto the dunes in front of the house. She twirled in place, her face raised. The sun glinted off her golden hair, her face lit up with a smile.

"She's the spitting image of you at that age," Dad said, grinning.

"Do you think so?"

"She has her own personality, that's for sure. But she reminds me a lot of you. And your mother, of course."

Bea loved that her father saw so much of Mum in her. And now in her daughter too. It was the best compliment she could get, as far as Bea was concerned. She missed everything about Mum. The shine of her hair under the sun's burning rays, the way her brown eyes twinkled whenever she said something mischievous or stretched the truth.

Dad had always said she couldn't lie between bedsheets, and Bea had never understood what he meant until now — her mother was guileless. She couldn't be deceptive, couldn't fake her feelings, and couldn't hide them either. Whatever she felt, they all knew. Thankfully, she spent most of her life happy, and passed that on to the people around her. Right up until those last years.

Bea took her eyes off the beach, and her beautiful daughter who was examining shells in the sand, to survey the cottage. It was in a worse state than she'd thought. The last time she'd visited, it'd been rundown. But now there were holes in the roof. The porch was rotted, and half of it had caved away. The paint had peeled from most of the walls that held only remnants of the pale sea green it'd once been.

"Wow," she said.

Dad stood beside her, tipped off his hat, and scratched his head. "Yep."

"It's going to take a lot of work, Dad. Are you sure you want to pour money into it?"

He shrugged. "What else do I have money for? I thought you might visit more often if you had a place to stay by the beach."

She inhaled a slow breath. "I might never leave."

He looped an arm around her shoulders. "That's fine by me."

* * *

Later on, Bea was at the local grocery shop buying some supplies to stock her father's pantry. She'd showered and changed into a pencil skirt, matching shirt and coat. Oversized sunglasses were perched on top of her head. She'd curled her hair and put on lipstick. She might be in the middle of nowhere, but she should really still make something of an effort with her appearance even if no one would see her.

Dad wasn't used to having three people in the house, let alone a hungry teen. Honestly, she was surprised how well he'd done so far with his hosting abilities. When she was a kid, he wouldn't have known a spatula from a wooden spoon, yet he'd woken early that morning to make them pancakes for breakfast.

Things had certainly changed. Although she didn't want to put him out too much — they both hoped to stay with him a while and so would have to pitch in. She also needed dog food and treats for Fudge, who was due to arrive within the hour. It would be interesting to see how well the little pug adapted to life without fences and with the ocean so close by. She was nervous, to say the least.

"Nice to see you back on the island," said Doug, the cashier. She'd known him since she was a small child and had even worked for him for a while during her teen years. She'd been the worst checkout operator in town, but he'd never complained.

"Hi, Doug. It's good to be back."

"Staying with your dad, are you?" He pushed her groceries slowly over the scanner, one by one.

"That's right. Me and my daughter, Dani."

He smiled. "Oh, that's nice. I'll bet Elias is thrilled."

She nodded. "How's everything with you?"

"Can't complain. The fishing's been pretty poor now with the colder weather."

"Yeah, Dad said something about that."

"But business is good and Peggy has a new hip, so she's got a whole new lease on life."

"Wow, a new hip. Good for her."

"Modern medicine is a marvellous thing."

She paid for her groceries and carried them outside in two fabric shopping bags. There was a café next to the shop, so she set her groceries on the ground outside and went in. It would be nice to have something other than instant coffee. Dad wasn't exactly a gourmet when it came to the finer things in life like coffee and wine. She'd already stopped by the liquor store to stock up on her favourite beverages.

Her stomach grumbled. She should buy herself a treat as well. She rarely ever ate sweets, was always watching her weight. It was time to enjoy herself a little bit. Even though she'd moved to the island indefinitely, it still felt like she was on holiday.

"Can I help you?" A lady behind the short glass counter looked her up and down. She had a bottle-red bob and was buxom with an apron tied around her ample waist. Bea remembered her from years earlier. Her name was June

Clements, and she'd always been a grouch for as long as Bea could recall.

It'd seemed as though June had something against her as well, although Bea couldn't imagine what it was. She'd barely had anything to do with the woman over the years. And from what she recalled, her mother had been a friend of June's at one time. But they'd had a falling out. Bea still didn't know what it was all about, but June had never gotten over it. Now she was behaving as though she didn't recognise Bea, which was perfectly fine with her. She could be an anonymous customer and avoid the awkwardness of June pretending to be happy to see her.

Bea scanned the goodies lined up inside the glass case below the counter. There were cakes and biscuits—most looked homemade. What she really fancied was a pastry. She'd eaten a chocolate cream-filled croissant once when she was nineteen years old that she'd never forgotten. What she wouldn't give for one of those right now.

"You don't happen to have any croissants, do you?"

June's eyes narrowed. "Kra-sonts, did you say?"

"You know, the pastry?"

"Nope. No kra-sonts."

"Oh, that's a shame." Her stomach grumbled again, this time louder.

"Next thing, you'll be asking for a lah-tey." June laughed, a big belly laugh that shook her apron. She raised a pinkie in the air beside her face as though she was drinking tea with the queen. "Ooh la la." Then she laughed uproariously again before calling in another woman from the back to tell her all about it.

Bea's eyes widened. "Sorry, I..." She didn't know what to say to that. She turned and left the café, picked up her groceries and hurried across the street to her car. When she reached the car, she put the groceries in the boot, then leaned against the vehicle and let a giggle escape her mouth. It bubbled up from within, and she seemed powerless to stop it. She clamped a hand over her mouth and tried to hold it in, but it was no use. She giggled hysterically.

Between gasping breaths, she exclaimed, "Next you'll be asking for a lah-tey!" She wiped the tears from her eyes and sighed. "Welcome to Coral Island, baby."

She'd parked her dad's old station wagon next to the primary school and could see a group of kids exercising in the playground. A tall man with a whistle hung on his neck ordered them around. It had to be Aidan. From this distance, he looked exactly as he had when he was seventeen years old, only bigger.

She stepped closer to the short chain-link fence that surrounded the school grounds and watched. He noticed her almost immediately and waved. She raised a hand, embarrassed, and turned around to get into the car. But he called out her name, so she stopped.

He jogged over to the fence. "Hey, fancy seeing you again so soon."

"I was at the shops."

"Ah, of course. Stocking up on essentials."

"Also, I asked for a croissant at the café. Apparently, June Clements thought that was the world's funniest joke."

He chuckled. "Trying your luck, were you? I'm afraid you've stepped back in time, Rushton. We don't have those kinds of snobby pastries around these parts."

He hadn't called her "Rushton" since high school. Her surname had been printed on the back of the senior shirt, and he'd called her that as a pet name from the first day she wore it. It brought a deluge of memories flooding back.

"So I discovered. It seems they're not fond of making lattes, either."

He laughed out loud. "You really were hoping for a miracle, weren't you?"

"I'm dying for a coffee. Dad only has instant, and apparently the café doesn't serve anything else either."

"You can get drip coffee at the café, can't you?"

"Wow, my world has been shaken." She rolled her eyes. "The fact that you don't remember I hate drip coffee."

He laughed. "Of course I remember. I'm only teasing. Come over to my place tomorrow morning, and I promise to give you some good coffee. You can see my new house as well. I've got to go over there to put in some light fixtures anyway. But the espresso machine already lives there. I've got to have my coffee too."

"We have that in common," she replied.

"So, tomorrow?" He pressed his hands to his hips, squinting.

"That sounds really nice. I'd love to see what you've done with the place. Dani and I have committed to renovating Dad's old beach cottage, so I might get some ideas from seeing your new house."

"The one you lived in when you were little?"

"That's the one," she replied.

"I can give you plenty of tips, then. I've been through the wringer pulling this place together."

"I look forward to it." She gave him her mobile phone number and waved goodbye. He promised to send her the address, and they agreed to meet at eight a.m. It was Saturday, so he didn't have to be at school.

As he walked back to join his students, her heart skipped a beat. It wasn't a date—they were two old friends who wanted to catch up. There was nothing more to it than that. She really needed to stop reading romance novels. Nothing ever worked out so perfectly in real life. Her own marriage was evidence enough of that.

Eight

THE NEXT DAY started much the same way as the previous one had. Bea took a walk on the beach, but this time with Fudge, who'd made the trip to the island in his usual happy style. He'd sniffed out every single corner of the house and had run up and down the beach until he was utterly exhausted.

This time, there was no sign of Aidan, but there were a few swimmers in wetsuits doing freestyle along the shoreline. The waves on Coral Island never got much bigger than thigh height, and most of the time were knee height since all the Whitsunday Islands were protected by the Great Barrier Reef. Which meant surfing wasn't a sport that flourished on the island.

The lack of waves, plus the presence of deadly jellyfish for much of the year and the proliferation of reef sharks, was enough to dissuade even the most enthusiastic surfer. The mainland also had to contend with saltwater crocodiles, which thankfully weren't a problem on the island. The waters of northern Queensland had plenty of dangers to keep residents and tourists on their toes.

While Dad and Dani ate breakfast, Bea borrowed her father's old station wagon again and set up the GPS on her phone, then drove to Point Prospect. Butterflies buzzed in her stomach as the car inched along the road Aidan had given her as his address. It was silly to be nervous over seeing an old friend. Still, she was curious to know why he'd asked her over for coffee. Perhaps he was being friendly—neighbourly, even. After all, she had gone on and on about her coffee obsession.

She'd had a headache two days in a row and was looking forward to drinking a real espresso, maybe even a lah-tey. She chuckled at the memory of the exchange in the café the day before as she parked her car on the opposite side of the road to Aidan's mailbox.

His house was beachfront, located down a driveway that sloped away from the road to the right. She followed the drive and found a stylish and modern house built from aged timber with several different levels and artistically placed windows at the end of the drive. The house was surrounded by coastal gums, hibiscus trees, native orchids and various types of seagrass.

The entire garden was brand new, complete with round, white pebbles in the bed. There were no curtains or blinds on any of the windows. The sunlight shone right through and into the bare, white-walled house. The external walls were painted grey, and the roof was a charcoal corrugated iron. Bea smoothed down her skirt with both hands, drew a deep breath and rang the doorbell.

Aidan answered the door in a pair of board shorts, a long-sleeved cotton top, and with freshly washed hair, still slightly damp. He kissed her cheek and ushered her into the house.

"Welcome, come on in. What do you think?"

"It's amazing. I love everything about it. And look at that view!" She walked to the back of the house, where a kitchen and dining area led out to an enormous deck with a perfect view of the beach.

"I bought the land just for the view," he said, following her onto the deck. "I've wanted to live somewhere I could hear the ocean from my living room ever since I left home and moved to the city. I spent over twenty years listening to traffic instead of waves. And now I can hear the ocean all the time."

"I'm completely jealous," she said, leaning on the railing to stare out over the sparkling waters and golden sand.

"I don't know—your dad's place is pretty fantastic. There's nowhere else on the island like it."

"True, but it's not mine. It's his."

"Will you get something of your own?"

"I'm not sure what's going to happen. Once Dani and I renovate the old cottage, maybe she'll live there, maybe I will, maybe we'll both stay there together. It's hard to say. She's going through a bit of a life crisis, trying to figure out what she wants to do with herself. And I'm going through a divorce."

He leaned next to her, his forearms on the porch railing. "I'm sorry to hear that. I didn't know you were having marriage problems."

"It's recent," she admitted. "He met someone else. They're engaged. And I don't fit into the picture anymore." Saying the words that way made her heart feel heavy. Sadness ached in her throat.

"He's an idiot."

"I won't argue with that." She laughed.

"How about some coffee?"

She sighed. "That would be perfect."

They chatted while Aidan prepared the coffee. The coffee maker, cups and spoons were the only things set up in the brand-new kitchen. It sported grey marble bench tops, white cabinets and a large rectangular window that looked out across the sand dunes above a round natural timber table. The floor was light caramel-coloured timber that blended beautifully with the coastal style of the house.

They carried their mugs onto the porch and sat side by side looking out over the ocean. They talked about their hopes and dreams, families and favourite travel destinations. The conversation was easy and comfortable. It brought everything back in a rush of memories, emotions and affection all wrapped up as one.

Bea recalled why she'd fallen for him all those years ago. There was a spark of chemistry between them that was difficult to ignore. And even though talking had always been something the two of them had no trouble with, she'd wondered if the physical connection would still be there. She couldn't ignore the fact that he'd grown into a very handsome man.

He was fit and strong, tanned and tall. She was pale and a little dumpy. Her fitness came and went depending on the season and how motivated she felt. Lately, she'd done nothing more than take walks in the morning, and not every day. She felt very much like a middle-aged mum, while he was a glamorous former footballer.

The discrepancies between their life experience were a chasm she couldn't push aside. He wasn't interested in her as anything more than an old friend. He wanted to catch up, and she was glad. She'd missed him and all of her friends on the island.

* * *

That afternoon, Bea and Dani walked down to the cottage with a notepad and pen, a measuring tape and stepladder, and got to work. They examined the entire structure from top to bottom the best they could without injuring themselves by falling through the rotting floorboards and noted the measurements of each room. They jotted down what was needed, which was basically everything.

Dani even wondered out loud if they should price a bulldozer and entire rebuild just to compare it to the refurbishment costs. But Bea couldn't stomach the thought of her childhood home being demolished, so they pushed that idea aside for the moment and focused on how they could improve the place.

They'd need to replace the entire deck that wrapped around the outside of the cottage. The structure of the building seemed to be sound, but they'd have to get an inspection done by a contractor before they could say for certain. They'd decided to have a contractor do the bulk of the work while Bea and Dani made the decisions and supervised since the renovation needed was more extensive than any of them had realised. It would make the whole project much quicker and easier, and since the cottage was so small, Bea didn't think the costs would be prohibitive.

The roof and floor needed to be replaced, and everything would have to be painted. The kitchen was in terrible shape and completely dated, so that would have to go. Along with the bathroom. Bea thought they should extend the master bedroom and turn it into a suite. So they added that as an optional extra, if her father's budget could take it.

Once they were done, each covered in cobwebs and coated in dust, they sat on a rock at the edge of the beach and stared at the cottage.

"So much work," Dani said.

"But I really think it'll be worth it. This position is unbelievable. So close to the beach, with only a bit of shrubbery and the dunes in the way."

"I can definitely imagine myself living here. Although what would I do to make a living? I've got to get a job before I run out of money. I can't expect Pa to take care of me forever."

"I bet you could find something on the island without too much trouble," Bea replied, swatting at a fly.

"What about you? Are you going to look for work?"

Bea shrugged. "I suppose so. I'm taking a break first. I need to clear my head and think through some things. I'm feeling off kilter."

"Of course you are." Dani laced an arm around Bea's shoulders. "I hope Dad comes around."

"What?"

Dani faced her. "Isn't that what you want? Him to change his mind and take you back?"

Bea stared at the sand by her feet. Was that what she wanted? After everything he'd done, would she be able to love him again the way she had before? She didn't think she could.

"No, honey, I don't think that is what I want. I wish this whole thing had never happened. But I'm glad not to be in the dark any longer about it. I know this isn't what you want to hear, and I'm sorry that you're caught in the middle of it, but I'm ready to be out on my own. It's hard and I'm scared. I don't know what to do with myself, really. My whole life has been wrapped up in you and your brother and father. I gave every part of myself to being a wife and mother. Without that to keep me going, I have no idea how to get up each morning." She shook her head, her voice sounding hollow.

"But you do get up each morning."

"That's true, I do. I suppose I'll keep going the same way — simply get up and go on with my life. But it might take me a while to find peace with that."

"That makes sense," Dani murmured. "I don't really know what I'm going to do either. Although my problem is different to yours — I have so many doors open to me, I have no idea which one to walk through. What should I do, Mum?"

Bea hugged her tight, kissing her cheek. "I can't answer that for you, honey. But perhaps together we'll figure it out."

Nine

A SCRATCHING sound woke Bea late the next morning. She'd overslept and wouldn't have time for her morning walk. The scratching happened again, and she climbed out of bed to investigate. After opening the window, she looked outside to see a magpie walking across the roof of the back deck.

"Shoo!"

The bird looked at her with one black beady eye, moving its head up and down.

"Are you chasing birds now?" Dad asked, peering in through her open bedroom door.

"It woke me up." She pouted.

He laughed. "Time to get up anyway, I think. Besides, we have a visitor. So get dressed and come down for breakfast."

"Who's the visitor?" she shouted after him. But he didn't reply.

With a sigh, she padded into the closet to find some clothes to change into. Who would call at this time of morning unannounced? It was a bit rude. Unless something bad had happened. What if Harry was hurt? She hadn't spoken to him in a couple of days. When he was little, he'd clung to her as though he'd never let go, and now he never even called. When she spoke to him, it was because she picked up the phone and dialled his number, never the other way around.

She ran a brush through her blonde hair, noting the existence of a few more greys and that her hair was past her shoulder blades now. She'd have to find a hairdresser and get it cut soon. There must be one on the island, although she hadn't seen one lately.

She remembered Harry's first haircut. He'd always had dark brown luscious waves. Even when he was an infant, the big, soft curls had been there. These days they were much thicker and tighter, but then they'd been so soft and sweet.

He'd sat on the barber's chair with wide eyes, taking it all in. He didn't make a fuss. That wasn't his style. He'd always been such a sweet, easygoing boy. Unlike his sister, he didn't let the world know when he was unhappy about something, but took it all in stride.

She missed him so much, it hurt sometimes. She'd think of him, or a memory would flash across her mind's eye, and her heart would ache with a physical pain that she thought would never leave. But it did, and she was fine again. Usually she'd pick up the phone and call him when that happened, but most of the time he was in class or busy.

She was proud of him for moving out when he didn't have to and starting a life of his own. He could've lived at home to attend university, but wanted to be independent. It was harder on her than it was on him, since she'd given up her own desires to raise her children and to be a loving wife. Now that they'd all left her behind, she had to rediscover who she was and what her life should look like.

Downstairs, a clatter came from the kitchen, and the delightful scent of fried bacon hung in the air.

In the kitchen she stopped short when she saw her

brother, Bradford, seated at the dining table beside Dani. "Brad, wow. This is a surprise."

He stood, all six-foot-four inches of him, and offered a lazy smile, one corner of his mouth turned up, the other down.

"Hey, little sis."

"I'm the big sister," she objected.

"Not in size," he replied, coming over to hug her. His arms enveloped her and made her feel tiny.

"What are you doing here?"

"I heard you were in town and couldn't miss the opportunity."

"Did you take the ferry over from Airlie Beach?"

"I have my own boat," he replied.

Bradford ran a successful charter fishing company out of Airlie Beach. He'd trained as an accountant and had a natural business acumen that'd seen his company grow quickly.

"Of course you do," she replied. "How many do you have now?"

"We're up to twenty."

"Wow, amazing," Dani said.

"I can take you out in one sometime," he said, returning to his seat. "Show my little niece around the islands. I have a lovely catamaran that would be perfect. We can sail, swim, snorkel, even do a little diving if you have your license."

Dani shook her head. "I don't know how to dive. But I'd love to learn."

"That sounds dangerous," Bea said.

Bradford chuckled. "That's rich, coming from you."

"What do you mean?" Dani asked, her brow furrowed.

"Nothing at all. He doesn't mean anything. I'm starving. We should eat."

Brad arched an eyebrow at her, but didn't respond.

"Oh, come on. I'm not a little kid anymore. You don't have to protect me from all Mum's antics. I can handle it."

Brad raised both hands as if in surrender. "That's up to your mum. I don't want to cross any boundaries." He leaned over to whisper behind one hand. "Later, okay?"

Bea crossed her arms. "Anyway, do tell — how are you?"

"I'm good. How long has it been since we spoke?"

She calculated in her head. "I think it's three years."

His smile faded. "Too long."

She didn't want to talk about the conflict between them. Not now. There was enough going on in her life without Bradford making things more complicated. "But here you are, and we're about to have bacon and eggs with Dad's famous sourdough, by the looks of it."

Their father dished the food up onto plates. "Grab a plate while it's hot."

At thirty-eight years old, Bradford was seven years younger than Bea. She'd loved him intensely as a teenager, when he was still a little child. She'd helped him learn to tie his shoes, read to him at bedtime—did a lot of the things their mother would've done if she'd been well. But he'd changed in adulthood, and she wasn't certain how to communicate with him. He was hardheaded, and that stubbornness had caused her to walk away from yet another conflict.

When they were teens, she didn't want to be responsible for picking Bradford up from parties when he'd drunk too much to drive home. Hated seeing him throwing his life away and left it for her father to deal with. Bradford had pulled himself together and had become a success in his thirties. However, the two of them still didn't know how to talk about the hard things they'd been through or how to navigate the pain of the past.

They sat around the table and ate, talking about things that wouldn't cause a fight. Bradford spoke about his business and how well it was going. Dani updated him on her indecision over university, and he listened intently, nodding every now and then. He asked Bea about their house and her work, but didn't mention the divorce. She wasn't sure if Dad had told him, so she decided to raise the subject herself.

"I'm not sure if you know this, but I'm getting divorced."

His eyes widened. "Dad didn't say. I'm sorry to hear that."

They spoke about it in a bit more detail. Bea noticed that the pain had dulled a little over the past few months. Perhaps in time, she could remember what her husband had done without feeling as though someone was stabbing her in the heart.

"Sounds like it was a good idea to come home for a while." He reached out to squeeze her shoulder.

"Thanks. I think so too. Dani and I are headed down to the cottage to meet a contractor recommended by a friend of mine. You're welcome to come if you'd like."

"That sounds good. I'd like to see the old place. Who is this friend of yours?" His eyes twinkled. "Anyone I know? He wouldn't happen to have a football jersey hanging in the cupboard, would he?"

Bea felt herself blush. She wasn't a school girl any longer. "Yes, it's Aidan Whitlock, if you must know."

"How is he these days?"

"He's good."

"Looking good, or just good?" He winked.

She couldn't help laughing. "Both."

"Well, look at you..."

"I'm not even divorced yet, so don't you dare suggest anything untoward. Especially in front of Dani. We're old friends, nothing more than that."

"I'm only joking," Bradford replied. "Let's take a look at that cottage, and while we're at it, you can tell me all about Harry and how he's going."

* * *

They met Aidan and the contractor at the cottage two hours later. Aidan had worked with Brett O'Hanley on his house at Point Prospect and highly recommended him. Brett didn't usually do such small jobs as the cottage but was willing to do a favour for Aidan, for which Bea was grateful. She and Dani had a conversation with Dad after breakfast about budget and timing for the renovation work, and he seemed happy with all their suggestions and was confident the cottage rebuild would be worth it.

"So, what do you think?" Bea asked Brett after they'd shown him around and walked him through all the things they wanted to do.

"I think it's going to be a lot of work, but nothing we can't manage. I'll send you a quote in the morning, and you let me know if you want to go ahead. I have a few weeks available starting next week before I'll be busy with another larger project, so you'll have to move quickly if you want me to do it."

Bea thanked him and agreed to call him the next day with their answer. Once he'd driven away from the cottage, she shoved her hands deep into her jeans pockets and walked back to join the rest of the group.

Aidan was walking the property perimeter to help her figure out a fencing option. Dad and Brad were arguing over the best roof types, and Dani stood to one side staring at the cottage with an overwhelmed look on her face.

Bea sidled up next to her and peered at the cottage too. "You ready to do this?"

"What if we make the wrong decisions about roofing or kitchen bench tops? It's a big expense for Pa." Dani's face was pale, her eyes wide.

"If we make the wrong decisions, we'll figure it out. We can't go into this fearful about making a bad choice. Life is a series of risks, and if you never take those risks, you won't get anything done. Look at this cottage, for example. If we don't take the risk of making bad decisions fixing it up, it'll stay rundown like this forever and no one will get to enjoy living in it. But if we take a chance, dive in and make the best decisions we can, then at the end of the day, no matter how perfect it is, it will be a beautiful little cottage that someone can spend years enjoying."

"I suppose that's true."

"Perfect isn't the goal. Liveable is."

Dani looked at her, blinking. "Why do I always feel like I have to get everything perfect?"

"Because you're taking your eyes off the goal. You don't have to get a perfect GPA in order to do well at university. The point of university is to become qualified for a profession so you can make a living to support yourself and any future family. It's not to be valedictorian."

Dani's eyes glistened with tears. "I've been so afraid of failing."

"Is that why you left school, honey?"

"I don't know," Dani cried, wiping her eyes with her fingertips. "I know I don't want to be a social worker, but I also know I was constantly anxious. I did so well in high school, but university is a completely different thing. I felt like I was failing, even though technically I wasn't. And I had this feeling that I had to be perfect, to do everything better than everyone else, or I wasn't good enough."

Bea wrapped her up in a hug. "Oh, honey, I'm so sorry you felt that way. You don't have to be perfect, or good, or really anything at all. I'm proud of you for being you."

"Thanks, Mum." She sniffled and wiped her nose. "I have to stop being so hard on myself."

"That would be a good start. I should do that too." Bea chuckled. "We Rushton women are perfectionists, but perhaps you and I can finally break that curse."

"That would be good." Dani squeezed her hand. "Thanks for being here with me, Mum. I really couldn't do this without you."

"Nowhere else I'd rather be."

* * *

Later back at the house, Bea sat outside to watch the sun set with a glass of wine in one hand. She wrapped her cardigan more tightly around her body as the wind picked up and howled under the eaves.

"Can I join you?" Bradford asked, setting his beer bottle on the table and pulling a chair out to sit.

"Of course."

"It's a little chilly for me," he said, pointing to the woollen beanie on his head with one finger. He still wore board shorts and had a sleeveless fleece on over his T-shirt.

"Queensland winter clothes," she muttered, shaking her head.

He laughed. "Of course, I have the Ugg boots on as well." He raised a foot to show her.

She held up a similar boot. "Me too."

"So, tell me, sis. How are you really going?"

She frowned. "I'm coping, which is surprising to me. I honestly thought I'd fall apart, but I've been so busy getting the house packed up, selling it and moving to Coral Island that I haven't had enough downtime to let myself go."

"Maybe it's time to do that."

"Maybe," she agreed. "Although I don't think that would help anyone."

"You can't push through something like this. You have to feel it."

She rolled her eyes. "Did you learn that at yoga camp?" She often joked about his hippie past. While she was at university and getting married to start a family, he'd spent a few lost years travelling around the world with a backpack containing everything he owned. He'd done yoga on the beach in Bali and meditation in Costa Rica. He'd had all the adventures she'd have loved to have experienced but couldn't because she made the sensible, mature choices.

"I learned it from my psychologist."

"You have a psychologist?" Her eyes widened as she took a sip of wine.

"Don't mock it until you try it." He feigned humour, but she could tell he was offended by her tone.

"Sorry, Bradford, of course. I'm glad you've found someone to talk to. Just surprised."

He dipped his head. "I know I'm not exactly the forthcoming type. But I've found it helpful."

The sun dipped towards the horizon, sending shafts of pink and orange light shooting out over the ocean. The water appeared black as it surged towards the shore.

"Good for you. But I don't know how to allow myself to *feel* being rejected by my husband and losing everything I thought my life would be at this point. I don't want to," she admitted. "It's too much, too hard."

"I understand, but you have to try," he said.

"No, you don't," she snapped. "You've never had a real relationship in your life."

"My girlfriend left me a couple of years ago, and it was a difficult adjustment for me. That's when I started going to therapy."

"A girlfriend is a little bit different to a spouse of twenty-five years. We raised two children together," she huffed.

His nostrils flared. "I understand that, Beatrice. I'm trying to be sympathetic, and all you're doing is yelling at me."

"I'm not yelling!" she shouted. She set her wine glass on the table, and it sloshed over her hand.

Bradford walked to the back door, then swung to face her. "I don't know why you hate me so much."

He slid the door open and stepped through, then shut it behind him.

Tears slipped from her eyes and down her cheeks. She dabbed at them absently with one hand. Did he really think she hated him? The idea hurt her heart. She loved him, but for some reason she reacted negatively to him even when it wasn't called for, they'd lost their connection, and she didn't know how to get it back.

Ten

THE CONTRACTOR'S quote was within their budget, and both Bea and Dani were happy with him, so they returned the signed contract to his office the next afternoon in Kellyville, the small town by the ferry dock where most of the island's businesses and residential houses were located. He would begin ordering supplies right away and would start work the following Monday. Bea was excited to get things started.

In the meantime, she and Dani intended to scour the island's small number of shops to see if they could find anything to decorate the cottage. The rest of the items they needed would have to come from Airlie Beach or be ordered online. It took most of the week to do the shopping and sort out orders, but they had a lot of fun working together to find things that matched their shared tastes.

On Sunday, she and Dani made their way down to the cottage to get started on what they could do. They'd decided to demo the kitchen and bathroom so it would be ready for Brett on Monday. They'd borrowed sledgehammers, chisels and hammers from her father's shed and drove down the narrow dirt track to the cottage.

Dad had wanted to drive them, although he'd had trouble with his back so wasn't able to help with the construction work. But Bea had insisted he stay at home and take some pain killers. There was no point in him making things worse for himself.

It was late afternoon, and they'd only have a couple of hours of daylight to get the work done. But they could come back the next day to finish it if they needed more time. Bea wore denim overalls with a white T-shirt underneath, her hair tied back under a scarf. Dani was dressed in old jeans with a pink crop top and had her hair in a short ponytail.

It felt like they were headed to an adventure, something new they'd never done before. No one else would be helping them demo; they'd have to manage it between the two of them, and they were each a little nervous.

"Are you ready to do this?" Bea asked as they stepped out of the car.

Dani offered a hesitant smile. "I suppose."

"We could let Brett do it tomorrow."

"No, we can do this. Right, Mum?"

"Absolutely," Bea agreed.

They set their tools down on the rotting timber deck, then walked inside. They had to dodge holes in the floor and tread carefully to avoid plunging through to the sand-covered foundations below.

"We should start in the kitchen. It's the biggest job," Bea said.

With safety goggles and masks firmly in place and gloves on, they got to work smashing down the cabinets, walls and bench tops that would be replaced by the contractor. They intended to open up the downstairs living area, making the entire place bright and airy.

After an hour, Bea felt as though her arms would fall off any moment. She stopped what she was doing and leaned on the handle of her sledgehammer, puffing. "I need to take a break."

Dani wasn't puffing nearly as hard, but gave a brief nod. "This is a lot more difficult than I imagined."

"You thought it'd be fun, didn't you?" Bea laughed.

"Of course. Why not? Knocking down walls and destroying cabinets — what's not to like?" Dani grinned as they both went out to the porch and sat on the edge, legs dangling, to drink from their water bottles.

"I don't think I can lift my arms," Bea complained, raising one limply and letting it fall again to her side. "It's permanently stuck in this position."

"I know what you mean. Wow, I should work out more."

"Ditto." They were both covered in dust. Bea wiped her face with one hand, and it came away white. "Thank goodness we wore a mask and goggles."

Bea's mobile phone rang. She pulled it out of her pocket, and a cloud of dust lifted into the air around her. "Hello?"

"Hi. It's Preston."

Bea's heart sank. She should've checked the caller ID before answering. "Oh, hi, Preston. How are you?"

"Fine, thanks. Listen, the money came through for the house sale, and I wanted to check you got your share."

"I'll look later. I'm out at the moment. But thanks for letting me know."

"Are you okay? Where are you staying?"

Bea was surprised and pleased the children hadn't told him. "I'm on Coral Island with Dani."

"Oh." He hesitated.

"Are you in Melbourne yet?"

"Yes, we've found a house. Moving in on Wednesday next week."

"I'm happy for you." Her heart rate accelerated. Talking to him like nothing had changed was going to put her in a panic attack if she wasn't careful. She inhaled a slow, deep breath to calm her nerves.

"Thanks. Listen, I just wanted to tell you I'm sorry. I don't think I said that, or at least if I did, I can say it again. None of this is your fault. You've been amazing. I wasn't sure how you'd react, but you've been a rock throughout this whole process. I want you to be happy, and I hope you will be."

She bit down on her tongue. The things she wanted to say wouldn't be appropriate in front of Dani. Her cheeks flamed. "Thank you, Preston. I appreciate that."

"It's just that... Well, it's different to what I thought it would be. Moving on...is hard. I miss you."

There was a voice in the background, followed by a loud music blaring.

"Look, I've got to go. Sorry, Bea. We can talk whenever you like. I know all of this was very sudden."

"Okay. Bye, Preston."

She hung up the phone and stared at it, gaping. Had that just happened? Was Preston already beginning to regret his hasty decision to end their decades-long marriage? And what would that mean for her? Could she take him back after everything they'd been through — everything he'd put her through?

"What did Dad have to say?" Dani's eyes were guarded, her voice soft.

"Sorry."

"Huh?"

"He said he was sorry for what he'd done."

"Wow," Dani replied. "That's big."

"I'm still trying to process it. He never says sorry."

"Never," Dani agreed. "Not that I can recall, anyway. He must miss you."

"He said that too," Bea admitted.

"Does this mean you're getting back together?" Dani's eyes crinkled at the edges as a smile drifted across her face.

Bea didn't want to get her daughter's hopes up. She didn't know how she felt. Confusion, fear, pain, anger — those were emotions she could connect with right now. Decisiveness about the future — not so much.

"I don't know what it means, honey. But right now, I can't imagine us fixing our marriage. He had a long affair... That's not something I can easily put aside."

"I know, but you could forgive him..." Dani looked so hopeful, it broke Bea's heart.

She cupped her daughter's cheek with one hand. "I can forgive him, and I will someday. But that doesn't mean we'll be married again."

"You're still married now."

"You know what I mean." Bea's face was warm—her heart pounded. She was ready to get back to work. To do anything other than talk about her marriage with Dani.

She got back onto her feet, then grimaced at the pain in her arms and legs. "Come on, we have to get this finished. We can talk about my failed marriage another time."

They headed for the bathroom and got to work demolishing it. Bea's arms had recovered enough for her to lift the hammer, but it was hard going. After about ten minutes, they both stopped, puffing hard. Bea leaned against the wall and raised her goggles.

"I can't believe we're almost done."

Dani sat on an upturned bucket. "It's getting dark."

"We'll go back soon. We should put on our headlamps."

Bea had found headlamps in Dad's camping supplies in the shed and brought down two for them to use. They slipped them over their heads and switched them on. The light from Bea's lamp illuminated the hole in the wall she'd made with her sledgehammer. They were expanding the bathroom out so that it wasn't so dark and pokey, and she was looking forward to seeing the finished product. As her lamplight glided over the hole she'd made, something glinted in the wall recess.

She froze, then shifted the light back to that place and stepped forward to peer down into the inner part of the wall.

"What's wrong?" Dani asked, standing and moving closer.

"I don't know. I saw something in the wall."

"Really? What is it? A rat? Please tell me it's not a rat." Dani shivered.

Bea grunted. "It's not a rat. It's..." She pushed a hand into the wall, and her gloved fingers closed around the hard object. She pulled it out. It was a small fabric bag, wrapped around something. "This. I don't know what it is."

"Let's open it up."

Bea carried the bag out to the deck, and they both sat on the edge. She pulled off her gloves, shifted her goggles from her eyes and lifted the object out of the bag. It was a film canister.

"What's that?" Dani asked.

Bea chuckled. "Film... This is how we used to take photos, kiddo."

Dani leaned forward and stared at the canister. "Why was it in the wall?"

"No idea. Someone's clearly hidden it there for a reason."

"Sounds spooky."

"Not necessarily."

"Didn't Pa build this cottage?" Dani asked.

"No, he bought it from someone."

"How do we get the photos?"

"We'll have to find a place that develops film and see if they can do something with it. It's pretty old, by the looks of it."

Dani pulled her phone out of her pocket and searched for somewhere they could take the film. "This place, Eveleigh's Books in Kellyville. It says here Eveleigh is an avid photographer who specialises in film photography. I wonder if she would develop the film for us."

"Eveleigh... That might be the Evie Mair I've known since primary school."

"Could be."

"Let's finish this up, and tomorrow we can find her and ask."

Eleven

WHEN BEA WENT to the cottage the next day to meet the contractor, Dani stayed behind in bed. She had a cold, with a sore throat and temperature. Bea's glands felt swollen, but someone had to meet Brett, and Dad had gone to the mainland for fishing supplies he couldn't get on the island. So, she was the only one available to go.

She ate a quick breakfast, ran a comb through her hair and pulled a hat low over her eyes, then ran down the track to the cottage. She was puffing hard when she arrived and found Aidan already there.

With her hands on her hips, she heaved for breath. "What are you doing here?"

"Good morning to you too," he said with a grin. "I'm meeting Brett, your contractor."

"I'm meeting Brett too."

"I have to talk to him about something to do with a project I'm working on, and he said I should meet him here, as he doesn't have any spare time today." He faced her, blue eyes sparkling. "It gave me an excuse to see you as well."

Her heart skipped a beat. "How nice." She told herself he didn't mean anything by it.

They'd reconnected when they caught up over coffee at his mansion on the beach, but that's all it was. He was a famous ex-football player, and she was a dowdy housewife. He'd already left her once, there was little doubt he wouldn't have changed his mind.

As much as she could easily let herself get caught up in the fantasy of the two of them together, she was a married woman. She didn't know what might happen with Preston and was entirely confused about the whole situation. Did he want them to reunite? Did she? There was too much up in the air for her to be flirting with an old flame.

He laughed. "I didn't mean to make you uncomfortable. It's nice to catch up again after all this time. I missed seeing you."

She tried to act casual. "Oh, yeah. I know what you mean. In fact, I think I'm going to see Evie later today. She has that bookshop in Kellyville, right?"

His brow furrowed. "That's right. It's a little independent shop with all kinds of old, out-of-print or hard-to-find books, along with the latest blockbusters, of course. There's a café attached, although it's closed now, I think."

She hadn't been certain it was the same Eveleigh she'd known as Evie from their school years, so she was glad to have her suspicions confirmed. "Great. I'm hoping she can help me..."

"That reminds me. I brought you something." He walked over to his truck, pulled a dog-eared book out of the glove box, and handed it to her.

The title was *Moving on from Grief.*

She frowned, holding it up to him. "Grief?"

He shrugged. "It helped me a lot when I lost my wife.

There are different kinds of grief. I guess I figured divorce was one of them."

"Oh, I see what you mean. Thanks. I really appreciate it."

The fact that he'd thought of her meant a lot. She realised she'd avoided dealing with her feelings since she left Sydney. The pain and grief of losing her marriage after twenty-five years hadn't really struck her yet. She still felt as though she was taking an extended holiday and would go home to her normal life soon. But she wouldn't. Her normal life had been blown up. Her husband was gone. Her children had left home. The house had strangers living in it.

"If you like, we could get together and talk about it, after you've had a chance to read a few chapters. For me, talking helped, although I took a long time to get to that point. I don't recommend denial. It doesn't work well for anyone involved."

It was as though he could read her thoughts. She blushed. "Of course, you're right. I have to admit to being in a bit of denial still. Can't quite believe my husband has a mistress and has left me to go and live in Melbourne. It's all so fresh still, but I suppose it's been a long time coming. I must've been in denial for years not to realise that something was wrong. I can see it now, although it's painful to admit it."

"It's not your fault," he said softly, reaching out to squeeze her shoulder. "He should've talked to you if he was feeling disconnected."

"You're right, he should've. We spent so much time apart for years — me taking care of the kids and the house, him at work. We got used to it, far more than we should've. It became our normal. I suppose that's why it was such a shock to me — I'd lived up to the contract we agreed to, and I assumed he had as well."

"Fair assumption."

"It seems I was wrong. About a lot of things."

"We're all wrong at times. No one is perfect. But I hope that if I felt something was wrong in our relationship, I'd talk to you about it."

"I think that's where you and I went wrong all those years ago as well." She held the book to her chest. "We didn't communicate."

"I've always regretted that," he admitted. "I learned from it, though, and made sure my wife and I spoke openly about whatever was going on in our lives."

"When you left for Brisbane, we hardly spoke. It was as though you walked out on me without explanation."

Brett pulled up in his truck with two other utes behind him full of construction workers. The interruption was welcome. This conversation was getting far too personal too fast. Bea's heart rate was elevated and her cheeks flaming with heat.

"Good morning," Brett said, climbing out of his truck. He wore work shorts, a buttoned shirt with paint splashed on it and an Akubra hat.

"Good morning."

"Ready to turn this cottage into the getaway of your dreams?"

Bea smiled. "I can't wait."

* * *

Eveleigh's Books was a quaint little bookshop down by the water's edge on the outskirts of Kellyville looking out over the parklands that hugged the shoreline. It was painted in blue with lilac trim. The paint was chipped and peeling. There was a rusted steel statue of a pelican on the front porch and an old fashioned ship's wheel hung from the wall.

A bell over the door rang as Bea stepped inside. It was

darker inside the bookshop. The small space was crammed with towering timber shelves stacked with books. Several people sat on small chairs or in beanbags around the shop, reading. A woman hovered over a cash register, hitting buttons and sighing in frustration each time the machine beeped at her.

"For heaven's sakes!" she exclaimed.

She held a small white booklet in her hand and had reading glasses perched on the end of her lightly freckled nose. Her red hair curled in wild ringlets all around a pretty face. She wore purple overalls with a white singlet top beneath them and glowed with a healthy tan.

Bea walked over to her and waited patiently. The woman swore beneath her breath as the machine beeped again, then peered at Bea over her reading glasses.

"Do you know anything about cash registers?"

"Um, sorry, no. Not really. Although I'm sure we can figure it out. Do you mind if I look at the instructions?"

The woman handed the booklet to her. "Please, knock yourself out. I'm about to lose my mind."

"What are you trying to get it to do?"

"Open the cash drawer. That's all I want. I bought this thing today and set it up. The old one was broken, you see. But I can't open the cash drawer to add change. I've been having to do it out of an ice cream container all day long."

"That is frustrating," Bea admitted, skimming through the instructions quickly.

She reached over the machine and hit a button. The cash drawer flew open. "There you go."

The woman cocked her head to one side. "Show me how you did that again."

Bea showed her.

"Wow, thank you. I get so stressed, I can't think straight. Also my glasses need a clean. It's impossible to see anything through all these fingerprints on the lenses." She pulled them off and rubbed them against her shirt.

"You haven't changed a bit," Bea said.

Evie squinted at her. "Beatrice Rushton?" She grinned widely and rushed around the counter to hug Bea. "I can't believe it's you. I haven't seen you in years. You look so different."

"Not you." Bea laughed. "Your hair isn't quite as wild, but otherwise you're exactly the same."

Evie stepped back. "Let me look at you. Weren't you brunette the last time we caught up?"

"That's right — I had a dark bob. But I'm back to my original blonde now. Helps to cover the grey."

Evie laughed. "That makes sense. And I love it—it suits you. Come on out to the back. I'll get Janice to run the till and we can have a cup of tea."

Evie spoke to an earnest young woman with a brown ponytail, then ushered Bea out through the back of the shop to a small kitchen and sitting area. Bea sat at a round table while Evie rushed around the kitchen fixing tea and putting slices of cinnamon tea cake onto a floral-painted plate.

"This place is amazing," Bea said. "It has such a good feel."

"Right? I think so too," Evie said as she slumped into a chair beside Bea. "I bought it about five years ago from a lady who ran a crystal shop, and turned it into a bookstore. It was my dream after I spent years working as a photographer to raise the money to do it."

"I was here three years ago and didn't get a chance to stop at any of the shops in town, otherwise I'm sure I would've noticed this place. Do you love it?"

"I love almost everything about it. Paying the bills is hard, but I do a few jobs on the side here and there to keep the lights on. Cake?" She held up the plate, and Bea took a slice.

"This looks delicious."

"Thanks, I hope it is. I enjoy baking, but it's not my strong suit. I had a café attached to the bookshop, but I had to close it for lack of help. I couldn't keep the place running along with the bookshop and everything else. It didn't do very well."

"That's a shame. It's such a lovely venue."

"Don't know anyone who would be willing to run the place, do you?" Evie laughed, then took a sip of tea.

Bea's mind raced. She needed work—what better way to settle into life on the island than to open a café? She could bake everything they needed and put in a real coffee machine so she could finally get the coffee she loved. Besides, with the offerings available in Kellyville from the cafe down the road, she knew there would be plenty of people happy to see some competition in town.

"Actually... I'd love to do it."

"Really?" Evie's eyes widened. "Don't you live in Sydney?"

"I've moved back home," Bea replied, loving the way those words sounded. *Home.* It was a good feeling, coming back to the place she felt most like herself in all the world.

"Wow, that's a big decision. And how does your husband feel about that?"

"He's moved to Melbourne...with his girlfriend. I mean, fiancée. I keep forgetting to call her that—it feels so strange. Silly me." Bea bit off a piece of cake. "Mmmm... Yum."

Evie leaned back in her chair. "Wow, I'm sorry. I put my foot in that."

"No, you didn't. It's fine. The sooner people find out, the better. I've hardly had a chance to work through it myself, so I probably should talk about it. They say avoidance is bad, right?"

Evie chuckled. "Apparently, although I find it works wonders for me."

"If you're open to the idea, I'd like to look around the café, and we can see if we'd be a good fit for each other. I ran a small catering business in Sydney, and I've organised plenty of events and functions over the years. I know I have the experience to run a café, and I'd love to try."

"I think it's marvellous," Evie said, beaming. "I can't imagine a better person to run it. I remember even in high school, you were a good cook. You used to make cakes and biscuits and bring them to school to share."

"Really? I'd forgotten all about that."

"Yes, plus you were great when we all tried to start that landscaping company — you organised us all and kept the accounts. We mowed people's lawns for an entire summer before folding because of squabbles over splitting the revenue. Our very own workers' revolt."

"Those were good times," Bea said. "Thanks for reminding me. My husband tells me I'm an airhead."

"I hate to be rude, but your husband sounds like a jerk."

Bea laughed. "It turns out, he actually is."

Evie laughed along with her. "I'm not going to push because this is a big decision, but I think we'd be great business partners. If you took it on, the café would be yours and you could pay me rent. Other than that, it would be up to you to manage the place and make it work. I won't have any input into the business. I have all I can take with the bookshop and my photography."

Bea sighed. It sounded perfect. Exactly the kind of thing she was looking for. "I'll get started on it as soon as we finalise the paperwork. I'm so excited."

"Me too. In fact, we should all have a get-together to celebrate."

"All?" Bea asked.

"All the girls from high school. Taya Eldridge and Penny St James live on the island too. Taya has an inn on the other side of the island. And Penny runs a wildlife rescue down the road from Taya's. We all catch up whenever we get the chance."

"I had no idea the entire gang was back on Coral Island. I've missed so much."

"You kind of drifted away and lost touch," Evie said, her eyes warm.

"I'm sorry," Bea said. "I should've made more of an effort."

"It's okay—life happens. Anyway, they'll be thrilled to see you. We're having dinner together on Tuesday night. You should come."

"I'd love to."

"Perfect. I'll let them know."

"I'm looking forward to it. Actually, I came down here to talk to you about something in particular." Bea reached for her handbag and pulled out the film canister, setting it on the table between them.

Evie picked it up and turned it over, her brow furrowed. "Where did you find this?"

"Inside a wall at the old beach cottage my dad owns. We're renovating it, my daughter and I, and this was sealed up in a fabric bag inside the wall cavity."

Evie's brows arched high. "Really? Well, isn't that an interesting little mystery?"

"I know. I can't help being intrigued. Why would someone put a roll of unprocessed film into a wall?"

"Your family has owned the building for a long time, right?"

"Yes, but it was built by someone else. Dad bought it from a man around the time I was born."

"That would make this film..." Evie rolled it around in her hands, examining the wording on the outside. "At least forty-five years old."

"Maybe fifty." Even as she said the words, Bea found it difficult to believe them. It was a long time for a roll of film to be encased in a closed space.

"Wow."

"I saw online that you do some photography. I was wondering if perhaps you would be able to process this, and we could see what's on it."

Evie smiled. "Well, you came to the right place."

Twelve

BRADFORD'S TRUCK was in the driveway the next day when Bea came home from a full day's work at the beach cottage. She sighed as she pulled the station wagon into the barn and turned off the ignition. She was exhausted, covered in paint dust.

All she really wanted was to climb into the enormous claw-footed bathtub in the ensuite off her old bedroom with a giant glass of red wine and look out the portrait window over the beach while she soaked and felt sorry for herself.

She was supposed to be going out to dinner with the girls from high school as soon as she'd showered and changed, but she wasn't sure how to get to the Blue Shoal Inn. She'd only ever been there with her parents as a child and vaguely recalled a narrow, winding track somewhere through the centre of the island. She'd have to ask Dad for directions. Hopefully, the old station wagon would manage the trip.

Dani was still unwell and had been tucked beneath the covers with a fever when Bea left that morning. She'd called to check on her at lunchtime, and Dad said he was feeding her chicken broth while she watched a movie in the living room.

At least she'd managed to emerge from the bedroom. And so far, none of them had caught the flu from her. Bea assumed that's what it was, since she had all the symptoms.

It often seemed that when a person slowed down after a period of stress, they managed to catch something. She was only now beginning to realise just how stressed and over-whelmed her daughter had been while studying at university. All this time, she'd believed her to be fine and completely in control. But apparently that'd all been an act.

She trudged up the stairs and kicked off her muddy boots outside the door, then stepped into the warm interior. Dad had been reading a newspaper in his favourite armchair. He'd fallen asleep with it open between his two hands, his light snoring filled the silence. Dani lay asleep on the couch, with the television screen stuck on a frozen image.

When Bea sat down, he opened his eyes and licked his dry lips. "There you are."

She smiled. "You were really out to it. How's the back?"

He grimaced. "A little better, I think. The medicine helps. But I'm struggling to turn my head much from side to side."

"That's hard, I know."

"How did it go at the cottage today?"

She shrugged. "Good, I think. It's slow going and hard work. I'm aching all over. But I'm loving it at the same time."

"I've been thinking about that roll of film you found in the wall yesterday."

"Oh?"

"The family who sold it to us was related to that woman who runs the local café — June Clements."

"Really? I always thought you bought it from someone on the mainland."

"I'm not sure where he ended up, but he was married to June. And the funny thing is, we only found out about the place because your mother and June were friends. But soon after we moved in, they stopped talking over an argument they had. I still don't really understand. Your mum was a complicated woman."

"Interesting... I wonder what it was all about."

Dad shook his head. "There was a lot going on back then. But I wonder if those photos belong to the fellow who sold us the house. And if they do, we could probably ask June to get in contact with him. She might know where he is now. He lived on the island for a long time, but I haven't heard anything about him in years."

"Good idea," Bea replied. "Thanks, Dad."

"You know, I'm proud of you," he said suddenly.

Bea blinked. She hadn't expected the kind words, and they brought a rush of emotion. "Thanks, Dad. What for?"

"You're strong, and you handle whatever life throws your way. You don't let it get you down or bury you. Your mother was a wonderful woman, but she didn't know how to deal with her emotions, or with hardship or stress, the way that you do. I'm glad you're here."

Bea reached out a hand to squeeze her father's. "That means a lot to me, Dad."

"And the offer still stands — I can take out that Preston fellow anytime. You just say the word." His winked.

"Even with your bad back?"

"A bit of anti-inflammatory medicine and I'm good to go."

She shook her head, laughing even as the tears welled. "That's good to know, Dad. I'll keep it in mind."

"You and Dani can stay as long as you like. Family sticks together through the hard times." He offered her a half smile. "This is your home."

"I'm grateful. I honestly don't know where I'd have gone if it wasn't for you. Coral Island feels more like home to me than any other place has. I'm only realising it now. I wish I'd understood that years ago."

"It wouldn't have changed anything," he said. "You're a loving and loyal woman. You'd have stayed with him even if you'd known."

"Perhaps you're right," she replied, knowing deep down that he was. Even if she'd had the foresight to see where her marriage would end up, she'd have stayed to do whatever she could to save it. And maybe nothing would've been different than it was now.

Dad stood with a groan and straightened his back. "I'm going to take a hot shower and see if it helps ease a bit of the muscle pain." He shuffled towards the master suite.

Bea flicked off the television and pulled a small throw rug up over Dani's legs. With a yawn, she wandered into the kitchen and put the kettle on to boil. While she was fixing herself a cup of instant coffee, hoping it would taste better than it had the day before, she noticed Bradford sitting out on the deck, talking on his phone.

His tall, gangly frame didn't quite fit in the slouching Adirondack-style chair with its bleached timber frame. A beer bottle stood on the table beside him. She pushed open the back sliding door and stepped outside. The wind whistled around the eaves. The hum of the ocean filled the air, and the sweet scent of salt filled her nostrils.

He told the caller goodbye and put down his phone, glancing at her from where he sat. "Hi, sis. Did you have a good day on the tools?"

She took a seat next to him. "It was fine. We got a lot achieved."

"That's good to hear."

"You still angry at me?"

He shrugged. "I guess so. But I won't hold it against you."

She chuckled. "Thanks for that."

"You're welcome. I see Dani isn't feeling well. Anything serious?"

"Just the flu."

"Well, I'd better steer clear. You know how sick I get when I catch anything."

"Man flu, I know. It's truly tragic." She rolled her eyes and took a sip of coffee.

The sound of a vehicle pulling into the driveway caught her ear. Soon after, there was a knock at the door.

"I'll get that," Bradford said.

"Thanks. I'm not sure I can stand." Her legs were stiff, and her back ached. She couldn't remember the last time she'd done so much physical work. She'd spent the day sanding and knocking down walls, digging holes in the garden and mixing concrete.

She knew she should leave the hard work for the labourers she'd hired, but there was something so satisfying about getting out there and putting her own strength to the test. She had to work out some of the frustrations that'd been building inside her in recent weeks, and this seemed like the perfect way. Although now she was paying for it.

Bradford poked his head out the door. "I'm going to town to pick up dinner, but you have a visitor."

When Aidan stepped through the doorway and onto the deck in a pair of dark jeans and a freshly ironed button-down shirt with an open jacket, his hair neatly combed back from his face, she startled. She was a complete mess. The embarrassment at being caught in her work clothes and covered in dirt, dust and grime from head to toe washed over her. She hated to think what her hair looked like. And the overalls she'd sported all day weren't exactly flattering.

"Oh, hi," she said, her cheeks flushing.

He bent to kiss her cheek, and she found herself stammering. "I wasn't expecting you. Was I? Did we have plans? I must've forgotten."

He laughed. "No, we don't have any plans. But I ran into Evie, and she said you were driving over to the Blue Shoal Inn for dinner with Taya and Penny. So, I thought I'd offer to take you. The road is pretty bad. We've had some rain recently, and they haven't fixed it yet. We can take my four-wheel drive, if you like."

Her heart skipped a beat. "Wow, that's so kind of you. Yes, I'd love that. I haven't bought myself a car yet, so that would be great. Thank you for thinking of me."

"Good. I'm glad to help."

"I wish I could ask you to stay for a meal, but I'm afraid it's not up to me. Taya and Evie organised it between the two of them."

"Not a problem. I have a meeting over that way, so I couldn't eat with you anyway."

"Oh?"

"I'm investing in a new property they're building nearby. Something small, only a half dozen units, but I need to meet with the developer."

"Wow, that sounds like an amazing project. Just a *little* bigger than my beach cottage."

He laughed. "I guess so, although I'm impressed with what you're doing. The cottage will be amazing after you're done, if you manage everything you've told me you're planning."

"So far, so good," she replied. "Can I get you a beer?"

"Thanks. That would be great."

She tried to stand and fell back into her chair with a grimace. "Give me a minute. I'm a little stiff after today."

He jumped to his feet. "Stay where you are. I can find the fridge."

He was back in a moment with a cold beer in one hand

and a bowl of pretzels in the other. "I found these in the cupboard, too. I hope that's okay."

She grabbed a handful as he set it on the table and ate them ravenously. "That's perfect. I'm starving. I forgot to pack myself a lunch with everything else that's been going on. At the rate I'm going, I'll lose ten kilograms before this renovation is over."

He laughed. "You certainly don't need to."

She cocked her head to one side. "Now, that's dishonest. But seriously — there's a decided lack of food in this house, and I'm spending all day working physically. I've never really done that before. Unless you count chasing after toddlers all day and doing housework. Still, the busiest time of my life was almost two decades ago now. I rarely do anything more difficult than a day in the garden or a workout at the gym. It's embarrassing to admit." She gulped a mouthful of coffee to wash down the pretzels.

"I know what you mean. I used to be so fit, playing football and training every day. Now, I spend far too much time on my computer or making phone calls. My life is very different these days."

She wondered how buff he must've been before. She couldn't imagine how much more chiselled he could be.

"How long will you stay with your dad?" he asked, munching on a pretzel.

"I don't know. As soon as the cottage is habitable, I'll move down there. I can't wait, actually. It's going to be gorgeous. And I'll be close enough to see Dad whenever I like. We're thinking of getting some two-way radios."

"You know they have these amazing things these days called mobile phones that let you call people?"

"You're hilarious. I know we could use our phones, but it might be fun to use radios. Dad will love it. He's always talking about going backpacking and hunting for his food and building shelters and things like that. He misses his old adventures with his mates."

He drank a mouthful of beer. "We all pine for a little adventure at times."

"You're right. All these years, I thought I was happy. That there was nothing missing from my life. But I'm beginning to realise I was settling for what I thought was best for everyone else in my life. I put aside what I wanted and instead focused on my husband and children. Now that they're gone, I have no idea how to be me anymore." She laughed, but inside she felt emptied out, and there was a dull pain in her chest.

"You're still in there. You haven't really changed," Aidan said softly.

"I suppose that's true. Although I feel pretty lost."

"Not surprising, given the circumstances. And your family isn't gone. They're in a different season of life, but they're still around. I bet they miss you too."

She swallowed as she met Aidan's gaze. His eyes were soft, and his mouth curled up at one corner into a half smile. Their history was full of memories, laughter, adventure and fun. But there was heartache as well. She'd given up on him when her mother died. And then he'd walked away without explanation to play football.

She felt herself getting sucked back into his orbit. It seemed impossible to be around him without wanting to be closer, to spend more time in his presence, to know him more. But she couldn't do that.

She was still married, even if they were separated. She didn't know what the future held or how her life would look a month from now, let alone a year. And with Aidan, there was no such thing as a simple relationship — no matter how appealing that might sound.

"I hope they miss me. Although, I have to figure out who I am now without them in my life on a daily basis. Dani is still here, and we're planning on living in the cottage together. But I get the distinct feeling that she really only needs a rest and some time out from the stress of the city life, and she'll be headed back there again before too long."

"Has she said that?" Aidan asked.

"No, but I know her pretty well. I think she's exhausted and she's putting too much pressure on herself. She's in the wrong degree program, and she hates to make mistakes or fail. But I'll have a talk with her and get her thinking about other options. She's going to be fine."

He smiled. "You're a good mum."

"I used to think so."

"You are. Your kids are lucky to have you."

"Thank you."

"You're welcome."

"I'm going to take a shower and will be ready to go in a few minutes." She stood to her feet and busied herself tidying up the outdoor table, moving coasters around and throwing leaves and sticks away. She didn't want him to see the tears in her eyes.

Her husband rarely said anything positive about her role as wife and mother. He didn't seem to value the one thing she'd put all her energy into. Having Aidan tell her she was a good mother meant more to her than she could express. But she didn't want to cry in front of him.

Instead, she'd go out to dinner with some old friends — she'd laugh and have a good time and forget all about the fact that her marriage of a quarter of a century was over and that her husband had started a new secret life that didn't include her or their children.

Thirteen

AIDAN WASN'T EXAGGERATING about the drive to the Blue Shoal Inn. The road was narrow and unpaved, and recent rain had left it with enormous potholes that the four-wheel drive had to crawl through.

Bea held onto the handle above the passenger door for dear life. "How does anyone ever make it to the inn alive?"

Aidan laughed. "Mostly they catch a boat or fly in. There's a small landing strip close to the village."

"So, people don't use this track?"

"Only locals. I'm surprised you don't remember it."

"Vaguely, and I don't recall it being quite this wild."

"It was always this bad, but kids tend not to remember the worst of things. They're called rose-coloured glasses for a reason."

She grimaced as they bounded into a new pothole. "I think you're right. I can't remember much other than the sand, the sun and the waves. We had so much fun in the ocean back then, it was almost all I thought about. Besides the sadness, of course."

He hesitated. "Yes, besides that. I always wished I'd been able to do more to help you through that."

"There wasn't anything anyone could do." She inhaled a slow, deep breath. It felt good to get that out. None of them could've done anything more than they did. She wasn't sure she'd ever admitted that before.

Until Preston told her he wanted a divorce, she'd lived most of her life under the illusion that she had some kind of control. But the truth was, she didn't. No one could control the surging ocean of life. It carried people where it willed, and sometimes all a person could do was splash around in search of a life preserver and then hold on tight.

"Still, I should've been there for you. I was in over my head. I didn't know how to be present in someone's grief. I wanted to do something, but really, all you needed was for me to be there. And I wasn't. I've always wanted to apologise for that — so here's my apology. I'm sorry I wasn't a better friend when you lost your mum."

A lump formed in her throat. She coughed to mask it. "No need to say sorry. You were a kid. I get it. You had other things going on in your life. No one else could really understand what we were going through, and I shouldn't have expected you to. I blamed you for not being around at the time, but now that I've raised kids through that age, I'm actually surprised how much of a support you were. Most teen boys would've run a mile long before you did."

Within half an hour, they pulled into the village of Blue Shoal on the opposite side of the island to Kellyville. It faced the open ocean but was protected by the Great Barrier Reef. The blue-green tint of the water looked like a postcard as it licked the long, white sandy shoreline.

At one end of the village stood an old blue inn. It was three stories tall, with white trim. The blue paint was faded and peeled away in places. The garden was a little overgrown. But otherwise, it looked much as Bea remembered it from her childhood. Back then, there hadn't been much more to Blue Shoal than a jetty, a small marina, the fish processing plant, a few quaint houses and the inn.

Now there were several small resorts, a large one under construction, a collection of upmarket shops and boutiques, and dozens of holiday homes. The inn was an elderly relic of yesteryear, standing vigil against the beach and glinting beneath the warm winter sun.

"I really love this place," Aidan said, putting the vehicle into park.

They climbed out and stood side by side, watching the sun setting over the ocean. The sky turned pink in a sudden flood of colour. The ocean fell into shadow, surging dark against the shore.

"That's amazing," Bea said. "I forgot how fantastic the sunsets are up here. It's nothing like this in Sydney."

"There's nowhere else like it."

They stood that way for several long minutes, watching the sun ease its way into the ocean. Bea's fingers brushed against Aidan's, and a jolt of heat flashed through her body. She crossed her arms over her chest, anxious not to give him the wrong impression.

"I should go," he said. "I've got to get to my meeting. I'll pick you up around ten?"

"That's perfect. Thanks for driving me. The road was even worse than I'd expected. I don't think Dad's station wagon would've made it."

"My pleasure." He walked away in the direction of the village.

Bea knocked on the door of the inn, then noticed it was open and pushed her way inside. There was a small reception counter on one side with a bell on it. She picked up the bell and rang. A young woman with blonde hair hurried out from a back room, tying an apron around her neat waist.

"Hi there. Can I help you?"

"Beatrice Rushton... I'm here to see Taya Eldridge."

"Of course, Ms Rushton. Please come with me. Ms Eldridge is expecting you in our private dining room."

"Wonderful."

Bea followed the woman through a large living area full of plush seating and lined with bookshelves stacked with hardcover books. There was an enormous fireplace in the centre of the room. On the other side of it, a spacious dining room dotted with round tables filled with inn patrons and decorated with cosy throw rugs on window seats and swirling blue and gold wallpaper. The back of the dining room looked out over the ocean through large picture windows. The light from the sunset gave the entire space the tone of an old-fashioned photograph.

Past the doorway to the kitchen and into another smaller room, Bea found herself surrounded by familiar faces.

Evie hurried to embrace her. "There you are! I'm so glad you came."

Taya Eldridge was a tall woman with long, sleek brown hair that hung straight in a bob that brushed the top of her shoulders. Her makeup was impeccable and her figure lithe. She offered Bea a smile over the top of an enormous glass of red wine.

"Beatrice Rushton, what a surprise to find you back on the island. You didn't change your name to something else, did you?"

Bea gave her a hug. "No, I added my husband's with a hyphen but didn't ever fill out the paperwork to make it official. As it turns out, that was a brilliant idea. Now I don't have to change it back."

"Well done, you," said Penny St James, a short, curvy

woman with honey-blonde curls that looked as though she'd stepped right out of a surf magazine. She kissed Bea on the cheek.

"Taya, this place is beautiful. It's hardly changed. I'm so glad you bought it — I'd hate to see it fall into disrepair. It's an institution on this island."

Taya's nose wrinkled. "It's not in great shape, but I do love the place. I've got renovations planned, but I'm waiting for the bank to approve my loan."

"And what are you doing with your time these days, Penny?" She faced her old high school friend with a smile.

"I set up a wildlife refuge over near that old beach house my family owns. Do you remember it?"

"Of course—we had a lot of fun over there. Snorkelling, fishing, swimming... Some of my favourite childhood memories were at your beach house. A wildlife refuge — that sounds amazing."

"It's fantastic, really. I started out as a marine biologist years ago in Cairns, then spent some time overseas. But I couldn't stand being away from home. I got a grant as part of the restoration of the Reef by the state government, and I spend my days tending to and caring for fish, sea creatures and other wildlife that are injured or in need of care. I couldn't imagine doing anything else these days."

"That's so perfect. You were always taking care of one stray or another in high school."

All of the women laughed at that, remembering the boys Penny used to date.

"Now, come on. The men in my life weren't all that bad. Were they?"

Evie grimaced. "Do you remember Sammy Taylor? We all went out for pizza one night, and you had to cut his pizza into squares for him and pay for his meal because he forgot his wallet."

Penny burst out laughing. "I'd forgotten all about that. Perhaps it's best that I didn't get married then, given my taste in men."

The four women spent the next few hours talking over old memories, eating the delicious food prepared by the staff in the kitchen next door. The noise of the dining room was blocked out by the closed door, but every time a waiter came through it to deliver something to their table or to clear a plate, the sound of happy patrons wafted in.

"You certainly seem to have a full house tonight," Bea said as she set down her napkin with a satisfied sigh.

"It's surprising how busy the place stays through winter— I think because our winter months are so pleasant. It rarely gets cold, and most of our rain happens in the summer months, so winter is basically a long string of warm, sunny days for people to enjoy."

"It's perfect," Bea agreed. "The exact right place to start again."

"I'm glad you're getting the chance to rebuild yourself," Taya said, dabbing her mouth with her napkin.

"And the cottage," Evie added.

"Which cottage?" Penny asked.

"Do you remember my family cottage, near our house?"

Penny nodded. "Oh, yeah. Of course."

"I'm refurbishing it, with the help of my daughter, Dani, and with my dad's money."

"Gotta love Dad," Evie said with a grin.

"My dad is great. I can't believe I didn't fully grasp how great he was before now. He's really been there for me in a non-confrontational kind of way. He's there without asking questions or probing. I can talk to him about anything I like, but he never pushes me. I've avoided him and this island for so many years. It hurts my heart to think about how lonely he must've been."

"I've seen him around the place, and he seems happy enough," Taya said. "He has a good group of friends who go fishing and four-wheel driving together. They often stop by the inn for a meal on their travels."

"Really?" Bea was glad to hear it. She wanted to believe that her neglect hadn't caused her father too much pain. She hadn't seen his friends in the time since she returned to the island, but perhaps they were staying away to give him space with his family.

"Don't beat yourself up, Bea," Evie said. "We all push away from our families in our youth. Then we come back when we sober up and realise what's most important. It's a normal rite of passage — stupidity and rebellion followed by repentance and reconciliation."

Bea laughed. "I guess that's one way of putting it."

"Oh, I wanted to let you know I've been investigating the best way to process your film."

"What film?" Taya asked as she set down her dessert spoon and pushed the half-eaten cheesecake aside.

"I found a roll of old film in a wall cavity at the cottage. I have no idea who put it there or what's on the film, but Evie is going to process it for me so we can find out."

"It might be completely destroyed. There's no way of knowing whether that bag was able to keep moisture out of the film all these years. And the temperature around here gets pretty hot. But it looks like it's a black-and-white roll, so there's a good chance it's in decent shape."

"That sounds interesting," Penny said after sipping her brandy. "It's like one of those old mystery movies by Alfred Hitchcock or something."

Bea's stomach tightened. It really was kind of exciting. What would they find on the film, and would it even be discernible after all this time?

"How old is the film?" Penny asked, pushing her blonde curls behind her shoulder.

"We can't say for certain," Bea replied. "But we've owned the cottage for around forty-five years. Dad thinks the cottage was only a few years old when we bought it. So maybe the photos are fifty years old? Something like that, anyway."

"Fifty-year-old photos that no one has ever seen. I'm officially intrigued." Taya's eyes narrowed. "But why would someone hide a roll of film in a wall cavity?"

"Maybe it's one of those time capsule ideas," Bea suggested. "A fun way for history to be preserved."

"I hope whatever it is doesn't involve any drama. I've certainly had enough drama to last me a lifetime." Taya shook her head.

"I was sorry to hear about your husband's death," Bea said, reaching out to touch Taya's arm. "I wanted to be here for the funeral, but I couldn't make it in time."

"Thank you, and I completely understand. You can't always get a last-minute flight to a tiny airport in northern QLD. But your flowers were appreciated."

"It must've been hard losing him like that."

"The hardest thing I've ever been through," Taya said, her eyes bright. "No one should die of cancer in their twenties. We were planning a family, but when we found out he was sick, we decided to wait. Of course, I was already pregnant, and we didn't realise it. Camden turns twenty next month. She's amazing, and she's studying in Cairns to become a chef at one of the big resorts there."

"Wow. You must be proud of her."

"I am very proud." Taya wiped her nose with her napkin. "She's the spitting image of her father. I only wish she'd had the chance to really know him."

They spoke in more subdued tones for a while about family and the passage of time. Then with a yawn, Penny announced it was time for her to go home and bottle-feed a bilby she'd rescued the previous week.

"Now that's a statement I never expected to hear," Evie said with a laugh. "Come on, I'll walk you out."

They all stood and made their way through the dining room, then out into the balmy night air. Overhead, a canopy of stars blinked bright in the clear sky.

"How did you get here?" Taya asked Bea.

"Aidan Whitlock drove me."

"Ooooohhh…" all three women said at once, facing her with wide eyes.

Penny grinned. "You wait until now to tell us this? When did you and Aidan get back together?"

Bea's face flushed with warmth. "We're not back together. He drove me out here because the road is a mess after the rain. I haven't bought a vehicle yet, and I can already see that I'll need something that can handle rough terrain when I do."

"That was very gallant of him," Taya said.

"Have you seen him lately?" Penny asked Taya. "He is still just as fine as he was in high school."

"Better, in fact," Evie added. "He's grown up well."

"Come on, ladies, no need to talk about him like he's a piece of meat." Bea's cheeks could set a match alight.

"It must be serious, then," Evie said with a whistle.

"Not at all. I'm still married and am broken-hearted. It will be a while before I can move on with someone else. And Aidan doesn't deserve to be mistreated, which is exactly what would happen if I jumped into something too soon. Besides, I'm not sure I'll even date again once the divorce goes through. I'm happy to be single for the rest of my life after this nightmare."

Taya, Evie and Penny all crowded in and threw their arms around her.

"We're just teasing you," Penny said.

"Of course we're teasing. You take all the time you need to heal."

"And being single is actually pretty fantastic," Taya added. "I've been single for almost two decades now. My life is very predictable, no heartbreak, no drama. I'm organised, on time to everything, and I get a lot done."

"Awww, honey," Penny said, kissing Taya on the cheek. "It's time we got you a date."

"Nope. I don't need a date. I need a life. Two very different things." Taya folded her arms.

Penny shrugged. "They can certainly overlap."

"I remember a time when you had a date every single weekend," offered Evie with a grin.

Taya shook her head. "It was during the era of dinosaurs."

"Come on, we're not that old," replied Evie.

Taya laughed. "It feels that way sometimes."

"You dated that guy with the skinny legs for ages in high school," said Bea. "What was his name?"

They all laughed together.

Evie's eyes sparkled. "I called him hairy legs."

"Ben, I think," added Penny.

Taya rolled her eyes. "Brent. His name was Brent. And you were all jealous of his skinny, hairy legs."

"Very jealous." Bea smirked. "Wasn't he the guy who always begged you to run away with him?"

"That's right, and you never did. Thank goodness." Penny leaned against the railing.

"I never understood it," said Taya. "We were so young. And I loved my parents. I had no desire to run away and be homeless. Looking back, I wonder if he had a bad home life to want something like that so badly."

"We all dated duds in high school." Penny sighed.

"Except for Beatrice," Evie said.

"Yes, all duds except for your Aidan," admitted Taya with a nod in Bea's direction. "He's a keeper, that one."

"I'm surprised none of you has asked him out." Bea's face flushed warmer still. "You're all single, and he's an eligible date. There aren't many of them on the island."

"We couldn't do that — girlfriends stick together," Taya replied.

Bea's throat tightened as she ducked her head. Her friends from high school had more loyalty to her than her own husband had. If only he'd considered her feelings before he'd cheated. She blinked away tears, then looked up at the circle of smiling faces around her.

"Well, thank goodness for friends," she said. "I've neglected you terribly, but I'm so glad we found our way back to each other again. It's as though almost no time has passed at all when I'm with the three of you."

Fourteen

"WHAT ARE you going to do about that husband of yours?" Dad's question at the breakfast table the next morning surprised Bea.

She was in the middle of a mouthful of cornflakes coated in honey when he asked it, and she almost choked. So far, he'd been very quiet about the whole divorce thing and hadn't asked about it, but of course it couldn't last. At some point, she'd have to think about the answers to those kinds of questions for herself and share them with others as well.

She swallowed. "I honestly don't know, Dad. I suppose we're getting a divorce. He asked for one, and he hasn't changed his mind as far as I know."

"Are you taking his calls?"

She grimaced. "Not exactly."

"How do you know he hasn't changed his mind, then?"

"Fine. If he calls again, I'll speak to him. I'm sure there are things we have to work out, but I've been avoiding it and spending all my time renovating instead. It's far more rewarding."

Dad chuckled as he spread Vegemite on his toast. "Of

course it is. It's easy to throw yourself into a project. Projects don't talk back and they won't break your heart. But you'll have to face him at some point, Sugar Pie."

"I know, Dad."

"If you ask me, you're better off without him. But it's not up to me."

"Thanks, Dad. I'll keep that in mind."

"You were always too good for that city slicker."

"Really?" Bea arched an eyebrow. This was the first she was hearing on her father's opinion of her husband.

"Yes. I never said anything about it because I didn't want to push you further away than you'd already run from me and from our family. Mum wouldn't have wanted that, so I stayed quiet. But he wasn't good enough for you then, and he definitely isn't now. Any man who'd do what he's done..." Dad waved his knife around. "Doesn't deserve you."

"Well, I happen to agree with you on that, Dad. I still don't understand what he was thinking. We were a family, the four of us..." She swallowed around a growing lump in her throat. "I suppose that doesn't mean as much to him as it does to me."

Dad rested a hand on her arm. "It means everything, and if he doesn't appreciate that, then he's an even bigger fool than I thought he was."

Just then, her phone rang. She pulled it out of her back pocket and stared at the screen.

"Speak of the devil." It was Preston.

She walked to the back door and answered as she stepped onto the porch. "Hello, Preston. How are you?"

"Thanks for picking up Bea. I'm well, thanks. You?"

It was surreal to hear his cheery voice on the other end of the phone, talking as though nothing had gone wrong between them.

"I'm great." She tried without success to keep the sarcasm out of her voice.

He cleared his throat. "Right, fine. Well, I think it's time we got together to talk through our divorce. Don't you? I'd prefer to keep the lawyers out of it if we can. They're so expensive, and I'm sure we can work it out fairly between the two of us. What do you say?"

She ran a hand over her face and groaned silently. There were about a million other things she'd prefer to spend her time doing than to sit down with her husband and talk through their divorce settlement. Pushing splinters beneath her fingernails came to mind as one possible option.

"Uh, yeah, sure. Of course, we should do that."

"Great. How about tomorrow?"

"Listen, Preston, I'm not really close by. I'm still on Coral Island with Dani and Dad, so it will take me a minute to get there."

He paused. "Oh, I see. I didn't realise you'd stay so long."

"Yes, I've moved back to the island."

"Permanently?" His tone was laced with disbelief.

"Yes, it's permanent." That was the first time she'd admitted the move was anything more than a temporary fix, an in-between step to getting her life back on track. But there it was. The words hung between them like a balloon waiting to be popped.

"Oh, wow. I wasn't expecting that. I thought you loved Sydney."

"No, *you* love Sydney. I loved you and wanted you to be happy, so I embraced our life there."

"Why didn't you say anything?"

"Because our family was the most important thing to me. I knew it was best for the kids, would give them the opportunities they deserved, to be in the city. But now I'm questioning all of it. Maybe I've been wrong and should've thought of my own needs more. Certainly, no one else will do that for me."

He coughed. "Well, I don't know if that's true. I've certainly done my best as a husband and father..."

"I don't want to get into an argument with you, Preston." She'd never spoken up to him like this before, and it felt good. "I'll come to Sydney next week, and we can work everything out."

"Ah, okay, then. I suppose I'll see you next week. I'll be in Sydney for a series of meetings on Wednesday. Does that work for you?"

"Wednesday is fine. See you then."

She hung up the phone, then stared at it for several minutes. How would this work? What would it be like to divide up an entire life? They'd already sold the house and split the proceeds. But there were so many other things they had to consider — their real estate and stock portfolio, the furniture, the artwork, the priceless collection of sculptures that Bea had spent countless hours researching and accumulating over the years. What about the photo albums and home videos? How could anyone divide up a lifetime of memories and senti-mental bits and pieces?

Back inside, Dad was washing dishes in the kitchen sink. "Everything okay?"

She nodded. "He wants to talk about the divorce settlement."

"Are you going to ask for alimony?"

"I hadn't thought about it."

"You should, you know. You spent a lifetime raising his children and gave up your career to do it. Meanwhile, he makes a fortune in his job and retirement savings because he had your support at home, and you're left virtually unem-ployable."

"Gee, thanks, Dad. When you put it like that, it sounds so warm and fuzzy."

"You know what I mean." He wiped his hands dry on a tea towel and faced her. "Don't let him get away without contributing something to you and the kids."

"I'll think about it. Did I tell you about the café idea?"

Dad's brow furrowed. "What café idea?"

"Evie has a café attached to her bookshop. She said I could have it and run it. I just have to pay her rent."

"Is that what you want?"

"The idea is appealing. I didn't come here thinking I'd stay on the island. But now... I don't know. I've felt so at home here. I have friends here. And now the opportunity to open my own café, something I've always wanted to do. The beach cottage is coming along nicely and is going to be gorgeous— I'm so excited to move into it. Things are looking up."

He smiled, crossing his arms. "Sounds like it's all coming together. Don't forget, though, that it hasn't been very long since your husband walked out on you. Maybe you shouldn't be making any big decisions for a while."

His words irritated her. Preston was no longer in her life. They'd sort out the divorce settlement, and then she could put him behind her for good. Even thinking the words stirred a vat of grief in her belly. Maybe she was moving too fast. But that's just how she operated. She was a doer. She didn't sit around stewing or wondering—she got in there and made things happen.

It was what she'd done on the PTA when they needed a new school hall, it was how she'd managed the fundraiser for the local choir to get a tour bus, and it was how she'd tackled her marriage separation — don't think, just do. It was almost a life motto.

"It's going to be fine, Dad. Maybe things are working out because it's time. I don't know. But I'm going to Sydney next week to meet with Preston. And then I'm coming back here to start my life afresh."

He leaned over to kiss her cheek. "I'm happy for you, love. And I'm glad you're finally home."

* * *

By the time Bea had caught the ferry the following Tuesday, the beach cottage had a brand-new kitchen and bathroom, she'd picked out the paint colour for the walls, and the landscaper had sent through the designs for the yard for her to look over while she was away on her trip. She'd signed a lease agreement with Evie for the café, and she'd asked Brett to look over the space and give her a quote for fixing it up the way she wanted it to be.

Everything was coming together, and she couldn't have been more excited to face the prospect of a future alone. If she must be alone, at least she'd have a café and a quaint beach cottage to dull the pain of her solitude. And with Dani helping her navigate each step of the process, they were closer than they'd been in years. They spent all day every day together — talking, laughing, swimming, walking, planning and enjoying life on the island. They'd even been snorkelling a few times, although wetsuits were definitely required in the cool water at that time of year.

She missed Harry, but had arranged to spend some time with him on her trip to Sydney. She couldn't wait to see him. On the video call they'd had the day before his hair was so long he couldn't see through it. She'd pressure him into a haircut if she had the chance, although she had to admit it looked cute on him, and at what other time in his life could he get away with looking like a human Labradoodle than during his university days?

While she stood on the ferry looking out across the ocean,

the wind buffeting her in her thin jacket, her phone rang. She pressed it to her ear with one hand, holding her hair out of her eyes with the other.

"Hello?"

"Hi, Beatrice. It's Aidan."

Her heart thudded against her rib cage. She'd told Evie that she was leaving town for a few days, but she hadn't called Aidan. She didn't want to explain to him that she was going to finalise her divorce. It shouldn't bother her to say the words. After all, he knew she was getting a divorce. But talking to him about it seemed wrong somehow.

"Hi. How are you?"

"I'm fine. Listen, I'm working over at Blue Shoal again today and wondered if you wanted to come with me. We could grab some lunch at the inn and say hi to Taya. Maybe we could have a swim after. I know it's cold, but actually, the water is nice."

She groaned inwardly. It sounded like the perfect day. "Wow. I'd love to do all those things. But I'm on the ferry."

"Oh? Where are you going?"

"Back to Sydney, I'm afraid. I'll be gone until Monday. Maybe we can catch up next week?"

"Next week would be perfect. What's going on in Sydney?"

She hesitated before answering. "I'm meeting Preston to go over our divorce terms. We have to figure everything out before we make things official."

"That makes sense," he said. "Just a warning—he may try to hide some of his assets from you. I've seen it happen a dozen times with the guys I know."

Her stomach clenched. She hadn't even thought of that. Surely Preston wouldn't stoop so low. "I'm sure he won't do that."

"Have you kept a handle on your finances?"

His words made her anxious. "Well, yes. I mean, not exactly. I don't have all the details and figures, but I have a general idea of how things stand."

"I don't mean to upset you. I'd hate to see you taken advantage of."

"Thanks, I appreciate it."

"Next week?" he asked.

She pushed a smile onto her face. "I'll see you next week. I have my phone on me if you need anything before then." She grimaced at her own transparency. The last thing she wanted to do was to seem like a needy woman, begging for his attention. She was still married, and although he was being more friendly than she'd expected, he could clearly get a date with any woman he chose. It wasn't likely he'd want that to be Bea, especially given their history.

After she hung up the phone, she found a seat outside the ferry cabin and sat down. She pushed her hands into her pockets and let her hair blow wild in the wind. A seagull watched her from its perch on the handrail nearby. The ocean looked like jewels had been flung across its surface as the sun danced over the water.

How had her life gotten to this point? She had a crush on her old boyfriend—there was no point denying it any longer. Her husband had a fiancée. And she was on her way to dissolve the marriage she'd believed would last a lifetime. Tears drifted down her cheeks and were whipped away by the wind as the seagull looked on with its head cocked to one side.

Fifteen

THE RUSH and bustle of the Sydney airport was a shock to Bea's system after several weeks of quiet, lazy life on the island. People in business suits with laptop cases slung over their shoulders hurried here and there. They were pasty, pale-faced and stressed-looking, while she had a glowing tan and felt completely relaxed apart from the ball of nerves in her gut over the meeting with Preston the following day. But for now, she could push all thought of that confrontation aside and instead anticipate her dinner date with Harry.

She caught the train into the city and met Harry at his dorm room. He seemed happy to see her and pushed out of their embrace to look her up and down.

"Is this really my mother?"

She blushed. "What do you mean?"

"You're tanned and happy-looking. I mean, you always look great, Mum. But have you lost weight? And are these biceps?" He pinched her arms lightly.

She shrugged. "I've been renovating."

"You look good. Well rested. Younger, in fact." He winked.

She smiled. "You've always been a charmer. Are you ready to go to dinner?"

"Isn't it a little early for dinner?" He quirked an eyebrow. "It's not even dark yet. Or are we senior citizens now?"

"Fine, we'll have drinks and then dinner. Although I might have to eat something with the drinks because I missed lunch since I was on the plane and they didn't serve us a meal — can you believe it?"

"They only do snacks for short flights now. At least that's what I've heard since I never actually go anywhere." He picked up his wallet from his desk and shut the dorm room door behind him.

"You poor thing," she teased. "I suppose you'll have to save some money to go travelling."

"Oh, come on, Mum. Everyone else's parents just pay for them to travel."

"You know I'm not that kind of mother. At least, not anymore. I'm a poor island dweller now."

He laughed. "I guess I can spend my summer on Coral Island. I won't complain about that."

"Do you really think you'll come?"

"Sure, why not? I can swim, snorkel, fish with Pa. What's not to love?"

"I'm sorry I haven't taken you there more often. I know Pa misses you."

He shrugged. "No need to be sorry for anything, Mum. By the way, Dad seems to be trying to make up for lost time. I've seen a lot of him lately."

"Really? I thought he was living in Melbourne."

"I think he misses you and Dani. He comes to Sydney just about every week and always wants to catch up with me. Spends hours talking and then drives me home and gives me cash. I don't think it's working out in Melbourne exactly how he thought it would."

"Oh?"

"Look, Mum, I don't really want to talk about it. I feel like I'm betraying Dad or something. Let's get going. You're buying, right?"

* * *

The next day, Bea rose early in her hotel room and went down to the hotel gym to work out. She felt fitter and stronger than she had eight weeks ago when she'd left Sydney, rejected and afraid. Now her future looked bright, and she was ready to embrace it with open arms — part of that would involve taking the time to care for her own health rather than putting herself last.

Getting fit at forty-five was an entirely different thing to what it'd been in her twenties. She found the changes incremental and most of the time wondered if it made any difference whatsoever when she worked out. But now that Harry had mentioned how well she looked, she had to admit that her body had begun to change, and the thought encouraged her to keep going.

Already she missed the island and her friends and family there, but she was glad she'd had the chance to catch up with Harry. They were meeting later in the day to see a movie together, and then tomorrow they planned to go ice skating. It was better than when she lived nearby, since they were both willing to make the effort to spend quality time together rather than simply seeing each other when he came home with a load of laundry or an empty stomach.

After her workout, she took a dip in the heated indoor pool and swam a few laps, then stretched out in the sauna. It was utter luxury after days of tearing down walls, hammering, digging and moving heavy objects. Before that, she'd spent weeks cleaning out her house. She was so tired. And the sauna seemed to help work out some of the kinks in her neck and back that'd become lodged there during her labours.

She showered and went to breakfast in the hotel restaurant down in the lobby. She'd never eaten at a restaurant on her own before, so she brought a book with her. But she didn't need it in the end. She spent the entire breakfast munching on eggs Benedict, bacon and toast while watching the people who walked by, or sat at adjacent tables.

It wasn't humiliating like she'd feared it would be, but enjoyable. She was free to think her own thoughts without interruption while watching people come and go. There was something liberating about not caring what anyone thought of her while also enjoying freedom from anyone's demands.

If Preston had been there, she'd have had to listen to his endless business-related stories and his complaints about the staff, the coffee, the cold eggs and whatever else he happened to be upset about at the time. Instead, she pondered the meaning of life, considered how many women were truly naturally beautiful without the aid of makeup as they came in and out of the dining room, and thought about the fact that a smile was the best accessory a person could wear.

By the time she'd prepared for her meeting with her husband, she felt satisfied, rested and ready to face whatever happened. Her only hope was that Preston's fiancée wouldn't come. This meeting had nothing to do with her. It would be cruel of Preston to bring her. And no matter what his flaws might be, he wasn't a cruel man.

Her nerves began to buzz like butterflies in her stomach when she climbed off the subway and up the stairs at Wynnum Station. They'd planned to meet in a conference room at Preston's office, since neither one of them wanted to include lawyers in their discussions.

It was an overcast day, cold and dismal with a light rain

that threatened to freeze if the temperature dropped a few degrees. The outlook made her miss Coral Island and its warm sunshine even more. Especially when a frigid wind blew between the skyscrapers and through her coat, giving her goose bumps all over.

Preston was still in his office making calls when she arrived. His secretary asked her to wait in the sitting area until he was done. Bea mused to herself that nothing much had changed — she'd always had to wait for Preston to be done in the past, and it seemed that the waiting would continue. But not for much longer.

When he came out to greet her, she didn't know what to say or do. He held out his hand to her, then seemed to think better of it and leaned in to kiss her cheek, but she turned her head at the wrong moment and their lips connected. It was completely normal and natural and yet took them both by surprise at the same time.

"Oh, sorry. I suppose we can't really do that anymore," Bea said, touching her fingertips to her lips.

"Uh, yes, I guess not. We'll get the hang of this before too long, I'm sure." Preston laughed nervously. He seemed even more on edge than she was.

With one hand on her shoulder, he ushered her into a nearby conference room. They sat on opposite sides of a long table in black leather chairs. The walls were timber panelling, and there was an enormous television screen hanging at one end. It was sterile and unwelcoming. Everything about the moment felt bizarrely surreal to Bea.

Preston steepled his hands above an open laptop. "So, how are you?"

"Fine, thank you."

"How's life on the island?"

"It's great, actually. Much warmer than here."

He grunted. "Sounds inviting. You look good."

"Thanks. Dani and I have been working hard on the beach cottage. It'll be ready to move into within the next couple of weeks. I'm excited."

"Good for you," he said, then swallowed.

"You look great, by the way. Did I say that already?" He gestured towards her with one hand, then looked down at his computer screen.

"Yes, you did." She pulled her own laptop out of her shoulder bag and set it on the table. "I suppose we should get started."

"You know, we'll still see plenty of each other," he said, as though she hadn't spoken. "We have two children together. I'm sure we'll bump into each other at the holidays and for big events."

"Maybe, although I doubt your fiancée will want to spend Christmases in the cottage with me on Coral Island."

"You wouldn't come to Melbourne?"

Her eyes narrowed. "Why would I come to Melbourne for Christmas? We're getting divorced, Pres. That's what this whole thing is about, or did you forget?"

He sighed. "I didn't forget. I thought you might be able to put that aside for the good of the family. But I suppose not."

"The good of the family? Really?"

"Let's not start," he said.

"No, let's. Because I'm still struggling to understand how you could do this to our family, Preston."

"What's gotten into you? You're not usually this…"

"Feisty, strong-willed, determined?"

He shrugged.

"I know, I should've shown you this side of myself a lot more than I did over the years. But I thought if I was easy-going and gave you whatever you wanted, you'd appreciate and love me. It seems I was wrong."

"I did appreciate and love you. I still do... I don't know..."

She huffed. "You have a strange way of showing it."

"Nothing's turning out the way I'd hoped it would."

"I don't understand what you're saying, Preston." She pushed her laptop shut. "How did you hope it would go when you asked for a divorce?"

"I thought we could be friends. That you would stay in Sydney, we'd still see each other, the kids would have you here with them. Now that you and Dani are so far away, who knows when I'll get to spend time with either of you. Harry is the only one returning my calls. I miss you both. That's all."

"This is what you wanted, Pres. You wanted to tear our family apart, and you have."

"It's not what I wanted, but I'm stuck between a rock and a hard place," he shouted, slamming one hand down on the table. He composed himself. "I'm sorry. You're right—we should go through the list of assets and get everything resolved. That's what you came here for."

As they talked about furniture, knickknacks and investments, Bea couldn't help wondering what her husband had meant when he said he was between a rock and a hard place. Was he feeling pressure from his new fiancée to be give her more than he'd planned?

Watching him sweat as he ran over line items on a spreadsheet he'd put together, she couldn't help thinking that perhaps she was seeing him clearly for the first time in a long time — she'd overlooked his flaws for so long because she had no other choice if she wanted a smooth and conflict-free life. But now she didn't have to worry about that. He was no longer a part of her life. Or at least, not a big part of it.

All the irritations and frustrations about his selfishness, his lack of consideration, the way he never appreciated her and the effort she put into being a good wife and mother all came crashing in on her.

With her attention firmly back on the spreadsheet, she did her best to understand what he was talking about. She held a finger up to each line item and processed what he was saying.

"Hold on," she said, studying the line that showed their main bank account. "Are you telling me that after all these years of working, there's only two thousand dollars in our bank account?"

"That's right. We basically live month to month from this bank account. Anything extra, I've put into our stock portfolio."

"But that only has twenty thousand dollars in it. And I know you've made well over a half million every year for the past ten years or so."

"That's right."

"Where's the rest of that money?"

He shrugged. "We spent it. We haven't exactly had a moderate lifestyle, Bea. You know that. You're the one who decorated the house, booked the holidays and applied for the golf club memberships."

She frowned. It didn't make sense. Yes, they'd lived more extravagantly than they should've, but why was there so little left to show for all those years of marriage together? "If we were so low on funds, why didn't you tell me to slow down? You always acted as though we had plenty left over."

"I suppose I wanted you to be happy."

The sad thing was, she almost believed him. He'd lied to her for so long that she was used to accepting his words. But the furtive way he refused her gaze gave her the first glimpse into how she'd managed to overlook his lies by not paying attention. She recognised the look — had seen it before many times. And if she'd been more discerning, she would've known he wasn't telling her the truth much sooner.

She'd been irritated when Aidan insinuated her husband

might hold back money and not give her the full picture, but perhaps he'd been right after all. Preston was hiding something from her. He was lying to her again—she was certain of it. This time, she'd get to the bottom of it.

Sixteen

AFTER HER MEETING WITH PRESTON, Bea went back to her hotel room and spent the afternoon on her laptop investigating their financial position. The more she looked into things, the less it made sense. They'd lived extravagantly in some areas of their lives, but they'd generally eaten at home, so they didn't have a lot of other expenses besides private school fees and the occasional family trip.

In recent years, Preston had earned a large salary plus annual bonuses, and they'd paid off their home a long time ago. She knew Preston had invested heavily in a real estate portfolio, but according to his paperwork, they owned only three units on the central coast.

That couldn't be right because she recalled various conversations over the years about single-family dwellings and high-rise apartment complexes on the Gold Coast, among other things. She racked her brain, trying to recall the details of those conversations. Why would Preston lie about something like that? He had to know she'd figure it out and question him over it. Maybe that was what he wanted. Or perhaps they'd lost money recently, and he hadn't wanted to tell her about it. She only wished he'd be honest and upfront with her.

She called the bank and asked them about any other accounts that might be missing from the spreadsheet given to her by Preston, but they said they couldn't help her with any information on accounts where she wasn't a signatory. Did he have accounts in his own name that he'd kept her from seeing? That was the question, and the way things stood, she wasn't going to get any answers.

She called down for room service for dinner. Then stood to stretch the cramps from her back and legs by the large square window at one end of the small hotel room. She was surprised to see that it was already dark outside. No remnants of the sunset remained; she'd been so busy working on her computer that she'd missed the whole show.

The hotel room was on the twenty-fifth floor and looked across Darling Harbour and the outline of the cityscape, dark against the sky. Stars and moon were hidden behind dark clouds that hung low over the city, and the water appeared black as an oil spill below.

After doing an online search for the name she recalled Preston had mentioned to her a few times, she called their accountant and left a message. Perhaps she could say she needed to access copies of her past tax returns for her records now they were getting divorced. It wasn't likely the accountant would let anything slip about Preston's private accounts, but it was worth a try.

Room service arrived with a chicken parmesan, thick-cut chips and steamed vegetables, along with a small chocolate pudding with custard. She also had a large glass of red wine on the side and sipped it with eyes shut as she leaned back on the small sofa, the television set playing the news quietly in front of her.

Comfort food — she hadn't eaten anything so rich in a

while and was soon searching through her toiletry bag for an antacid. Food on the island mostly consisted of whatever fish, oysters or prawns Dad caught at the beach that day, along with vegetables from his garden or the local market. No wonder she'd lost weight since moving there. Her father had always been sun-kissed, muscular and athletic. She and Dani were on their way to becoming just like him.

When the phone rang, it startled her. She muted the television and answered.

"Hi, Harry."

"Hey, Mum. I thought maybe we could meet up for breakfast in the morning before class. I want to hear all about how your meeting with Dad went. Well, not really. I'd prefer to believe you're both still deeply in love and our family is whole and will be forever, but I'm trying to be a supportive son."

She hated what this divorce was doing to their children. They were adults now, so it wouldn't impact them the way it would've a decade earlier, but it still hurt. She could see they were both struggling with the way their family was being torn apart.

"Yes, breakfast sounds amazing. I'll have a swim at the pool here and then meet you at eight a.m. Where would you like to go?"

"There's a restaurant on campus that's pretty great. They have chickpea pancakes that taste almost like the real thing."

She crossed her eyes. "Um, delicious. It would be an utter shame to have the real thing, of course, because..." She shook her head. What was it about the younger generation that they didn't like anything real? It was always imposter versions of the real thing.

"Wheat, Mum. It's bad for you. Don't you know that?"

"Right. It only feeds the majority of the world's population cheaply and with all kinds of nutrients, but now it's bad. Gotcha. I will keep that in mind."

He laughed. "Oh, Mum, you're not keeping up with the latest trends."

"And for that, I'll be eternally grateful." She sounded grumpy. Looking into her finances, realising she had no clue what'd happened in her own financial life for the past two decades and that the man she loved was probably keeping something from her, had stolen the joy she felt earlier about her new life.

"Are you okay, Mum?" He was confused — Harry wasn't accustomed to hearing her like this. She'd put so much effort into always being the happy, bubbly, carefree mother that he didn't know this side of her. So many things she would change if she could do it all again — she would be herself in all situations so that her family got to know who she really was, warts and all.

This cardboard cutout version of herself that she'd served to them on the perfectly styled platter all these years had done nothing but cause a disconnect. Perhaps that was why Preston had fallen in love with someone else. No, she couldn't blame herself for that or she'd go mad. He should've talked to her if he was feeling disconnected. That wasn't her fault.

If she was completely honest with herself, she knew she had to shoulder some of the blame for their lack of intimacy in recent years. Regardless of her part in it, though, he was responsible for how he'd responded. She still couldn't get past the fact that she'd remained loyal to him even when he'd turned to someone else for comfort.

"I'm okay, buddy. I'm feeling a bit low because of my meeting with Dad — which you don't want to hear about, and I'll respect that."

"It's okay, Mum. You can talk to me about it if you want."

She was torn over whether to reveal her concerns to her

son. She had no proof of anything, and the last thing she wanted to do was to badmouth Preston to their children.

"I'm concerned Dad isn't being entirely upfront about our financial situation. But I have no proof of that, just a gut feeling."

Harry hesitated. "You should make sure, Mum. It's not right if Dad doesn't share fairly with you — everything we have as a family, the two of you built together."

"It's not that I care, really. I have enough from the sale of the house to start my business on Coral Island, and Dad's helping me with the cottage. But it's the principle — I'm sick of the lies. I want us all to be honest with one another. And maybe he is being honest, but I'm going to get to the bottom of it and find out what's going on. I hope that doesn't upset you. I promise to be kind and considerate in the way I do it."

"That's okay, Mum. The only thing that would upset me is if Dad's holding back. You're my mother, and I love you. I don't want you two to break up, but if you must, I'll support you in any way I can."

"Just promise you'll always be honest and communicate with your future wife." She sighed. "That would make me very happy."

"I promise, Mum."

* * *

The next morning, Beatrice swam in the hotel pool, then showered and changed for her breakfast with Harry. She decided to walk to the train station and catch the train to his university campus, since it was only a short distance away.

The sun was out, the rain clouds gone for now. The wind was brisk, and she shoved her hands deep into her coat pockets and hunched down low into the magenta scarf wrapped around her neck. Her hair was held in place by a knit cap that matched her scarf. Otherwise, the wind would've whipped it into her eyes as it whistled between the tall buildings and along the narrow streets.

The roads were clogged with morning traffic, and people strode quickly in every direction. She almost collided with a bike courier at a set of traffic lights, then hurried down a staircase to the subway and jumped onto the train before it pulled away from the station.

As she was walking to the restaurant, her phone rang.

"This is Frank Perdue, your accountant, Ms Rushton. I'm returning your call."

"Oh, thank you for calling me back, Frank. I wanted to talk to you about my financial situation. You may have heard that Preston and I have separated and are getting a divorce."

"I did hear, and I'm sorry for you. I know this is a hard time."

"Thank you. I appreciate that. The reason I'm calling is that I really don't have any record of any of my finances for the past twenty-five years. Preston always took care of that, and I know I'll need to have copies of my tax returns and accounts for my records going forward. I'm planning on buying real estate, maybe a car, opening a business... All of these things may require me to provide some evidence of my financial history. Can you help me with that?"

"I certainly can. I'll be happy to send over everything I have for you."

"Thanks, I'll email you my hotel address. If you can send it all by messenger or email before Monday, that would be much appreciated."

"Happy to do it. Is that all?"

She swallowed. "Well, actually — I'm a little confused about how many accounts and investments Preston and I have. He's given me a list, but I have a feeling there are some things missing."

The accountant cleared his throat. "Well, unfortunately I can only share with you the things that are in your name. I can't talk about Preston's personal accounts and investments."

"Even as part of the divorce settlement?" Bea asked, her eyes widening.

"I'm afraid so. Mr Pike has advised me to keep his financial affairs private."

"From his wife?"

"Look, I suggest you talk to him about this. I'm uncomfortable being put in the middle of it. By law, I have to do what my client has asked me to do. And Mr Pike is my client."

"So am I..."

He was clearly agitated, his voice gruff. "Actually, I've never spoken to you before now, Ms Rushton."

After she hung up the phone, she considered his words. Why hadn't she ever taken it upon herself to speak directly to the accountant? To find out about her own financial position? She should never have left all of that to Preston.

Even if he was trustworthy, it wasn't sensible. Anything could've happened to him, and she'd have been completely in the dark about their situation and what needed to be done to survive. She'd never put herself in that position again.

After breakfast, she returned to her hotel room and readied herself to go for a walk around the harbour. She needed to get out into the fresh air and clear her head to think about what she should do next.

Part of her wanted to let it go, start again and move on with her life without worrying about anything Preston had or had not done. But the other part of her didn't want him to get away with being dishonest, if that was even what was happening. She didn't know for certain.

Maybe what he'd said to her was right — they lived in such a way that there wasn't much left over. She should let it go and accept that he was telling the truth. After all, she'd trusted him for most of her life. Why would she stop doing that now?

He called her when she was stepping out of the lift, and she held the phone to her ear as she hurried out of the building and onto the street. The cold wind slapped her in the face, and she strode quickly, hoping the fast pace would warm her up.

"Hi, Preston. I hope you're well."

His voice was cheerful. "I hear you have questions about our finances."

Someone had spoken to him. Most likely the accountant, but possibly Harry. "How did you know?"

"Let's get together and talk about it," he said, avoiding her question. "Where are you now?"

"I'm outside my hotel, going for a walk."

"Meet me on Martin Place. We can have a coffee and talk this through."

"Okay, I can be there in half an hour."

"See you then."

She hung up the phone and shoved it into the pocket of her aqua puffer jacket. She was completely underdressed to meet Preston in her workout gear with a headband around her forehead, but it didn't matter.

They would meet, they'd talk about finances, and she'd go on with her walk. At least this way, she might discover what was going on without having to spend the entire afternoon huddled over her laptop in her hotel room.

Bea made her way to Martin Place and found the café where Preston had arranged to meet her. It was close by to the Lindt Café where there'd been a shooting years earlier. She remembered it like it was yesterday, and the thought sent a shiver through her body as she walked by.

The poor woman who'd died was around the same age as her and had been pregnant at the time. She recalled looking at her own pregnant belly with tears in her eyes, wishing such things weren't a part of the world she lived in.

But real life wasn't all sunshine and roses, as she well knew. Mothers died, marriages fell apart and honesty wasn't everyone's preferred policy. She had to face the truth — she'd ignored the signs that were right in front of her for too long. Maybe the trauma of losing her mother so young had pushed her to pretend that everything was okay.

If she ignored it, she didn't have to face it. But if she'd paid more attention to her husband and what was going on in their home and their marriage, maybe she wouldn't have found herself in this situation.

Preston sat at a small table in the back of the café, playing on his phone. He looked up when she walked in, and she thought for a moment that he'd aged five years in the time since their anniversary party.

She sat across from him. "Hi."

"Latte?" he asked.

She nodded. "On skim milk."

"I know." He went to the counter and ordered their drinks, then returned with her coffee and a tea for himself in takeaway cups. He set hers in front of her and sat down, smiling. "Some things never change. A large latte on skim milk for you, a black tea for me."

"And some things change when you least expect it," she quipped, surprised that he remembered her coffee choice since it wasn't so long ago he'd claimed not to know she was a coffee lover.

He dipped his head. "Touché."

She took a sip of coffee. "I suppose you want to know why I called the accountant."

"The thought crossed my mind."

"I want to get hold of all my financial records. I don't have copies of anything, and I'll need them moving forward."

"For what?"

Her eyes narrowed. "All kinds of things. Why does that bother you?"

"It doesn't," he said. "I'm surprised you don't trust me."

"I didn't say that."

"What do you need? I can get it for you." He watched her carefully as he drank.

She set her cup down on the table. "I want to get a complete list of our investment portfolio — every property, every account... All of it."

"I gave you that."

"It doesn't seem right to me. I'm sorry if it sounds suspicious, but I suppose after everything that's happened, it is hard for me to trust you."

"I wouldn't do anything like that, and you know it." His eyes sparked. "I still love you. I care about what happens to you. I'm going to make sure you're taken care of."

"You do?"

"What?"

"Still love me."

"Of course I do. None of this was my... Ugh." He grunted. "Anyway, what I'm saying is... You can trust me. I'll do right by you."

"I'm glad to hear it." Could she? Could she trust the man who'd secretly had an affair and announced his intention to end their marriage on the evening of their vow renewal? "Were you about to say none of this was your idea?"

He shrugged. "What does it matter now?"

"It matters to me. Whose idea was it?"

He ran a hand over his hair. "I have responsibilities."

"Two responsibilities, actually — they're both at university and they still need us."

"I can't abandon Geri."

"I get that you believe you owe her something, although I

don't agree. What I'm wondering is why did you put yourself in that position in the first place? Why did you feel the need to fall into someone else's arms?"

He met her gaze for the first time, his brown eyes full of pain. "We lost touch with each other. I'm not justifying it, but that's what happened. I was on a work trip, I was lonely and disconnected from you. You were so busy with the kids, so occupied with them and what was going on in their lives, it was hard for me to get your attention."

"That was my job. I'm a mother." A sob caught in her throat. Finally they were having a real discussion about what'd gone wrong in their relationship, and it had loosened the ball of emotions wound tight in her gut.

"I know that. I'm sorry... What more can I say?"

"I'm sorry too."

"For what?" he asked, brow furrowed.

"For leaving you alone in our marriage. For not being someone you felt you could talk openly to about what was missing."

"I didn't want to burden you. You're an amazing wife and mother. It was my problem, not yours."

"We were in it together." She shrugged, wiping a tear from her eye. "I'm regretful for my part in it."

"Thank you," he said. "I often wonder if I was too hasty."

She frowned. "What do you mean?"

"Maybe I shouldn't have ended things with you the way that I did."

She studied the lines of his face. So familiar to her and yet sometimes he seemed a stranger. "I don't know what I'd have done — whether I could've forgiven you..."

"Would you consider giving me another chance?" His face opened up. He looked young and vulnerable all over again like he had when they were just two kids in love.

"I'm not sure. I have a whole new life on the island. It's a lot to take in. I thought you'd moved on."

"I haven't," he admitted.

"We'd have to see a counsellor. I couldn't start things back up again the way they were. We need to get to the bottom of what went wrong before we could even consider trying again."

He nodded vigorously. "Counselling, yes, let's try that. I think it's a great idea. If it doesn't work out, we can go our separate ways, but at least we'd have tried. I know that's what the kids want us to do."

"And what about you?" she asked.

"I want that too," he said, reaching for her hand and taking it in his.

She stared down at their connected hands, her mind in a whirl. How had they gotten here? She'd never have imagined this was how their coffee catch-up would go. She'd come here with questions, and now even more of them buzzed around in her thoughts. But she owed it to herself and her family to see if they could salvage their marriage.

She nodded. "Okay, let's see a counsellor."

Seventeen

WHEN MONDAY ROLLED AROUND, Preston convinced Bea to postpone her flight. So she did. Instead, the two of them went to a counselling appointment. He'd managed to find a counsellor through a friend at work who'd had a cancellation and could slot them in at the last moment. Bea was nervous about the whole thing — she'd never much enjoyed counselling. It seemed invasive.

Telling your innermost thoughts to a stranger and having them ask questions like "And how does that make you feel?" and "What did you think of that?" It set her teeth on edge. But if that's what it took for Preston to rethink the destruction of their family unit, she owed it to her kids to give it a chance.

Bea met Preston outside the counsellor's office. He leaned in to kiss her, but she turned her head so his lips met her cheek instead. She wasn't ready to do what he was asking — they wouldn't get back together until she felt as though he'd changed and she could trust him with her heart and her family again. She wasn't even sure she wanted to. She'd had a glimpse of how life could be without him, and it beckoned.

Now that she was back in Sydney, it was hard to believe she'd spent the past two months on Coral Island — it was more like a dream than the reality of the bustling city where she'd spent all of her adult life.

She'd spoken to Dani that morning, who assured her the renovation would go on without her. They talked over paint selections and decided together what should be done. Dani said she was happy to coordinate with Brett and that Bea shouldn't worry herself — the cottage would still be there when she was ready to return to it.

There was an undercurrent of excitement in Dani's voice, and Bea knew she and Harry were both barracking for their parents to reconcile. The knowledge of that made her anxiety worse — she couldn't promise them a reunion, only that she would let their father have an opportunity to make amends. After that, they would both see if they were ready to give their marriage another chance.

The rapid about-face Preston had undertaken was confusing and a little concerning to Bea. Maybe he'd felt pressured to give his new fiancée the life she wanted. Maybe he'd changed his mind once he realised how much he'd missed Beatrice. Or perhaps there was something else going on she hadn't quite put her finger on yet. But whatever it was, she was determined to take things slowly and be more careful with her heart this time around.

"Please take a seat. I'm Juliette." The counsellor sat across from them. She crossed her short legs, her green jeans contrasting sharply with a bright orange silk shirt.

"What brought you in to see me today?" She smiled, glancing from Bea to Preston and back again, her heavily made-up eyes half hidden behind a pair of black-rimmed spectacles.

"We're separated," Preston began, in his most businesslike voice. "And we want to work through the issues that caused the separation in the first place. We'd like to give our marriage another chance."

"For the sake of our children."

"Our family," Preston corrected, reaching for Bea's hand.

"I see. Why don't you tell me what happened, and we can go from there?"

As Bea and Preston laid out the circumstances that led to their separation, her heart was squeezed from every side all over again. The more she thought about the years leading up to their split, the more regret she felt, realising how differently she would do things now given a chance at redemption. But was redemption even possible after everything they'd been through and all the pain they'd each experienced?

Hearing Preston's side of things was eye-opening, to say the least. She'd had no idea he'd felt the way he did in their marriage. She had to give him, and them, a real chance or she would only add to her list of regrets.

* * *

Three weeks later, Bea was still in Sydney. She'd found a room to rent from a friend of hers who had a fully furnished guesthouse available above the garage. They were away overseas, and Bea had promised to keep an eye on the place for them while she stayed there. The property was impressive, with a double tennis court, large in-ground swimming pool and extensive landscaping. Every afternoon, the watering system flicked on and sprinklers saturated the property — she'd been caught outside reading or walking more than once when she forgot to check her watch.

She and Preston had attended counselling sessions twice per week with Juliette and her garish-coloured clothing. Bea had come to love the woman, who rarely asked the kinds of questions that made Bea's skin crawl and instead listened with compassion and empathy to both their points of view in equal measure.

Bea felt as though they'd made progress, although readily admitted to both Preston and Juliette that she still wasn't willing to open her heart up to the idea of a reconciliation. The lack of interest surprised her. She'd loved Preston for so long, but couldn't put a finger on when that had become a habit more than a reality for her.

"Give it time," Evie had said when she'd confided in her friend. "There's a lot of pain involved."

But at this stage, she wasn't sure time would do much more than deepen her resolve to move on. During one of their sessions, she'd forgiven Preston for his unfaithfulness and the way he'd broken the news to her. They'd both shed tears that day. Still, it didn't change the way she felt about their marriage.

She longed to return to Coral Island and pick up her new life where she'd left it. It was as though she'd come alive when she moved there and was reunited with the people she knew were her true friends.

Aidan had called her several times since she left the island. Each time, she'd sat with her feet up on the balcony railing at the guesthouse looking out over the tennis courts, and they'd spoken for hours. A couple of times, they'd video called, and he looked happy. Although he did ask when she'd return to the island more than once during most conversations.

Getting to know him again, rekindling their friendship, was the one thing she looked forward to most each day when she rose from her bed. And that was what worried her. How could she work on her marriage when she was busy falling in love with another man? Could she really say she'd done her best and given Preston a chance when she spent the minutes checking her phone to see if Aidan had called?

The entire thing gave her a knot in her stomach.

A memory washed over her like a black and white movie. Aidan standing just inside her bedroom door, her laying on the bed on her stomach, arms folded beneath her chin.

"Say something," he begged.

She inhaled a breath, squeezed her eyes closed.

"You can't just shut me out like this. We love each other."

Inside, her emotions warred with her mind. People who loved her couldn't be trusted. Mum had opted out of their family. She didn't ask for permission, didn't think about how it would hurt them, didn't listen to their begging words for her to get help, to feel their embrace, to take in their affirmations. It made no difference. In the end she left and Bea's heart was torn into pieces. Aidan would leave too. He'd been signed to the Brumbies and he wouldn't come back. No one ever came back....

She rolled over and sat up. Glared at him. "Leave, I don't care. It doesn't matter. Nothing does."

He'd stared at her, with pain in his eyes, then shut the door behind him. She wanted to cry but the tears clogged in her throat as she listened to his footsteps thud down the stairs. Then he was gone.

The memory jolted a deep sadness loose within her. If only she'd said something different. If only things hadn't worked out the way they had. And yet she couldn't regret the series of events that brought her Dani and Harry. Life was a funny series of coincidences, impulses and mistakes that when added together formed a beautiful tapestry she could only appreciate by taking a step back. Perspective changed everything.

She walked out the door of the guesthouse and trotted down the stairs with a tennis racket beneath her arm. The cap on her head was a little tight, so she loosened it as she walked. When she reached the courts, she switched on the machine that flung balls at her—she had no idea what it was called—

and hurried to the other side of the net, poised and ready to return the ball.

One ball came sailing over the net, and she hit it. It bounced directly into the net and then rolled off the court. With a grunt, she spun the racket around and bent at the knees, ready for the next ball. It came more quickly than she'd expected and bounced off the end of her racket into the fence.

She groaned. "This is more frustrating than aerobics class." When was the last time she'd done one of those? They were all the rage in the eighties and nineties. But she'd never managed to be coordinated enough and found herself stepping on the toes of other people who were at the end of their grapevine while she was only at the beginning.

Her phone rang, and she hurried off the court, catching a tennis ball in her hip. With a grimace, she answered the call.

"Ouch! Yes?"

"Ouch? Are you okay?" Aidan's voice sent a thrill up her spine.

"I'm fine. A tennis ball to the buttocks never killed anyone."

He laughed. "That sounds dangerous. Where are you?"

"At home. I'm trying to improve my return, but I think I'm getting worse. Can you actually regress by practicing? Because I'm fairly certain that's what's happening to my tennis game."

"You're a scientific anomaly."

"I've always suspected as much." She grinned and settled onto the grass, her back against the fence. "How are things on the island?"

"Good. I stopped by your cottage earlier—it's looking fantastic. They're almost finished with the landscaping, and they've started on the paint. It's beautiful. I think you'll love it."

"Oh, good." She squeezed her eyes shut, trying to picture

it. "I would ask you to show me on the phone, but I want to wait until I'm there to take it all in."

He hesitated. "Listen, I know we have an unspoken agreement not to discuss it, but I was wondering if we could talk about what you're doing in Sydney. Just for a moment."

"Of course. That's fine." Her heart skittered in her chest. She'd avoided this topic with him, and he'd been gentlemanly enough not to pry until now. She didn't want to hurt him and wasn't sure exactly where things stood between them.

"Are you reconciling with your husband?"

She bit down on her lip until it hurt. "We're going to counselling."

"And?"

"And I don't know. He wants to get back together, and I'm giving him a chance to share his side of things with me. But I still don't have a fixed idea of what that will mean for us long term."

"Do you still love him?"

"I love him as my husband of twenty-five years and the father of our children. But I'm not sure I'm still *in* love with him, if that's what you're asking."

"Okaaaaayyy." He was clearly not satisfied with her answer and was unsure how to ask for more without being rude or crossing a line. She wished he'd simply jump over the line and push her for an answer.

She sighed. "I'm sorry I can't be more upfront with you. But I suppose it only matters to you if... Well, if..."

"Yes?"

"If you're more to me than a friend."

His voice was deep and soft. "I was beginning to think that's where we were headed. Now I don't know. I don't want to get in the way of your reconciliation with your husband. But I'm sitting here, on the island, alone and missing you, wondering if I'll ever see you again."

His words made her head spin. It was more than she'd expected. She couldn't believe Aidan Whitlock wanted to date her. She was a frumpy housewife who'd spent years honing the skill of keeping people out of her heart and avoiding true intimacy.

She'd never have believed this would happen if she'd said it to herself a year ago, but if there was one thing she'd learned in recent weeks, it was that she needed to open herself up to connection even if there was a chance she'd be hurt. Because the hurt could come either way, and in the meantime, she and her loved ones were missing out on knowing who she really was.

"I don't know what to say."

"Don't say anything. I wanted to get that off my chest. Now I have. You don't owe me anything—we haven't even spoken about this before. I'd much rather have had this conversation in person, but things being what they are, I suppose this is what we've got to work with. All I will ask is this—will you come back to the island sometime, no matter what the outcome of your counselling and reconciliation attempt, so we can talk for real? I think we owe it to each other to say the words face-to-face."

She sighed. "Yes, of course. I fully intend to come back to Coral Island. It's all I can think about lately. I miss it there too, and I miss you, of course. I know I shouldn't say that, but I can't help it."

There was a smile around his words. "I'm glad to hear it. I'll leave you alone, then. Let me know when you're coming home. We'll set a time to meet and talk."

When she hung up the phone, she couldn't wipe the smile from her face. She stood to her feet and hurried back around the net. Then she slammed the first tennis ball that came her way directly over the net.

Eighteen

IT WAS a Thursday four weeks later, and Bea had never been so bored in all her life. She didn't have to clean the guest-house because a cleaner came every Wednesday. The family had taken their dogs with them, so there were no pets to feed or care for. A gardener came twice a week to manage the landscaping and garden beds. And Harry was back into the swing of his semester, so he didn't have time for more than a couple of catch-ups per week.

Apart from her counselling sessions, she was completely at a loss for anything to do. She decided to get dressed up and catch the train into the city to surprise Preston for lunch. There was an amazing German restaurant on Darling Harbour that they both loved — Preston had always raved about the salted pretzels, and she loved the sauerkraut.

She called and made a reservation at the restaurant, styled her hair with a curling iron—something she rarely ever spent the time to do—put on makeup and her favourite warm suit with a pair of flats, and headed for the train station on one of the bicycles stored in the garage.

As she wobbled down the road, hunched over the handlebars, she was reminded of one of her first dates with Preston. They were so young when they met, neither one of them owned a car. He'd showed up at her dorm on his bicycle. She'd fetched her own bike from the garden shed, and they'd gone riding together through the tangled city streets.

They'd ended up in a park. She'd come off the bike and grazed her knees on some gravel. He'd lovingly washed the blood away with some water from his drink bottle and the bottom of his T-shirt. She'd never wanted the day to end.

Now she was on a bike once again, headed to town to surprise him. It was romantic and nostalgic, and she hoped he would be there. She should've thought to ask him about his schedule. He was in the Melbourne office some days and the Sydney office on other days. Thursday was a Sydney day, she was fairly sure, but not entirely certain. Even if he wasn't there, it would be nice to take a wander in the city and grab some lunch. If she stayed at the guesthouse any longer, she'd be certifiable by sunset.

The train ride into the city was uneventful. It was warmer out of the wind, and Bea peered out the window, imagining herself back on Coral Island, sitting on the cottage's front porch with a book in one hand and a glass of wine in the other. Perhaps she should return to the island for a week, just to get things in order with regards to the cottage and the café.

If she and Preston were going to make things work, would she have to give up the café? She hated to let it go. She finally felt as though she was doing something for herself, and now she wouldn't get the chance. She could try to convince Preston to move to Coral Island. She wasn't sure how that would work and couldn't imagine him living there.

She caught the elevator up to Preston's office and decided to bypass the busy receptionist with a telephone pressed to her ear. Instead, she hurried along the hallways, past the giant wall of windows that overlooked the harbour. Preston's office door was ajar, and his assistant wasn't in her usual seat. Bea walked to the door and gently pushed on it. She was about to call out his name when she heard his voice and fell silent. He was probably on the phone. She could let herself in to sit on the couch and wait for him to finish up whatever he was working on.

"I know it's a pain, but we've got to do this to secure our future."

Bea's ears pricked. Who was he talking to? A woman's voice murmured.

"I know, my darling," Preston replied, his voice muffled. "It's not long now. Everything will be sorted out very soon. I need a little time—that's all. You can go back to Melbourne and wait for me there. I won't be far behind."

The door swung open. Preston stood at the far end of the office, his arms around a woman. It was Geri. She rested her head against Preston's chest, her red hair spilling over his shoulder and down his back. Her green eyes popped open at the sound of Bea's gasp. She stepped away from Preston.

"Beatrice? I wasn't expecting you." Preston's face flushed red.

"I can see that." She pressed her hands to her hips. "I think it's time I got an explanation."

"I'll talk to you later," Geri said, flouncing out of the office with a glare in Bea's direction.

The imprint of the two of them wrapped up together in Preston's office knocked the wind from Bea's lungs. She gaped at Preston, feeling nothing but a sad emptiness. There was no passion left, no hurt feelings or love lost. Those had been chased away by Preston's first confession. Now all she wanted was to put it behind her.

"I suppose that makes my decision easier," she said.

Preston walked to meet her, palms raised. "That wasn't what it looked like. Don't get the wrong impression. We were saying goodbye."

"Why are you lying to me about her?"

His shoulders slumped. "What do you want, Bea?"

"I want us both to go on with our lives and be happy. And from what I've seen, you're pretending to want a reconciliation with me because you don't want me looking into your finances. I've never been unfair. I'm not trying to take advantage of you, Preston. I only wanted you to be upfront with me. If you'd have been honest, none of this would've happened in the first place."

He shrugged. "I've worked so hard..."

"We both have. In different ways."

He sighed.

She studied him — the hangdog expression, the slouched shoulders. He loved his money more than he had loved his wife. As far as she was concerned, he could have it. "I don't want anything from you. We can split the assets you included in the spreadsheet down the middle, and anything else is yours. You're far too caught up in material things, Pres. You always were. None of that ever mattered one bit to me. I don't care about it. I have everything I need back on Coral Island. I hope you'll be happy with Geri and your new life."

His eyes widened. "But Beatrice..."

"I'm done," she said. Then she spun on her heel and stalked from his office.

His assistant stood in the doorway, gaping. She grinned at Beatrice as she strode past and dipped her head in a brief nod. "Goodbye, Ms Rushton. And good luck."

"Thank you. You too."

Then she took the lift down to the ground floor and stepped outside into the frigid air. With her head tilted towards the sky, she grinned up at the clouds and tucked her scarf more tightly around her neck and chin. Then she headed for the subway station. She was going home to Coral Island.

* * *

Back at the guesthouse, Bea called the airline and booked the first flight north that evening. Then she called Harry to tell him goodbye. He said he'd visit during his next break from classes, and she promised to decorate a room for him in the cottage. She would miss her son, but other than him, there was nothing she was sad to leave behind.

She let Dad and Dani know she was coming. Then, her final call was to a moving company and arranged for them to transport her belongings from the storage facility to Coral Island the following week.

She'd spent every day in Sydney running, cycling and playing tennis. She was fitter and stronger than she could remember being at any time in her adult life. She was bored and listless, lonely and irritable — there was nothing she wanted more than to get back to the island, the renovation and Dani, her new café and the friendships she'd built since her return to her childhood home.

A knock at the door surprised her. She opened it to find a courier placing a box on the ground by the door. She signed for the package then carried it into the guesthouse and placed it on the dining table.

It was addressed to her. The return address on the label was for a shipping company in Airlie Beach. She frowned as she slid a knife under the tape sealing the box shut. Who would've sent her something from Airlie Beach? She couldn't imagine Dad would've sent something to Sydney knowing she was on her way back to the island soon.

Inside, there were several bags of coffee. The scent of the beans drifted up to meet her, and she squeezed her eyes shut to inhale with delight.

"Delicious," she whispered.

Whoever had sent it clearly had good taste in coffee.

There was an envelope in the box. She slid a finger under the flap and opened it. A photograph fell out onto the table. It was a picture of Aidan's smiling face. He pointed at a large, shining espresso machine on a clean marble kitchen bench top. The bench was deliciously stylish, and she admired it for a full minute before recognising it as the bench top she'd selected for the cottage.

She turned the photograph over and read the words printed there.

Dear Bea, this beauty is waiting eagerly to make your first coffee in your new cottage. I hope you like it. Your friend no matter what, Aidan xo

His thoughtfulness brought a lump to her throat. She wanted to call him and thank him, but decided to wait until she was home to see him in person. The gesture was something Preston would never have thought to do. Even when they were in love and spending every moment they could together, he'd never done anything so thoughtful.

It was simple, but it showed Aidan cared. Even if they were never anything more than friends, she knew Aidan was in her corner. He understood her, knew what would bring a smile to her face, and he was willing to go out of his way to make that happen. For her in that moment, after what she'd witnessed at Preston's office, it was everything.

* * *

It was late when she got to the island that night. She rode the last ferry under the starry sky. The gum trees that rose high and dark around the town of Kellyville swayed and rustled as she drove the station wagon, which Dad had left parked at the ferry terminal for her, back to the house.

Her father greeted her with a kiss and a sparkle in his eye. "It's good to see you, love. I'm glad you're home. Sorry it didn't work out the way you'd hoped it would. But he's a lout if he can't see what's right in front of him."

"Thanks, Dad. I'm exhausted. I think I'll go right up to bed. Is Dani in?"

"She's having dinner with friends in Kellyville."

"I'm glad she's found some people to connect with. Please tell her I'll see her in the morning if you're still awake when she comes home."

Bea lugged her suitcase up to her bedroom, took a hot shower and collapsed into bed. Her throat was sore and her glands were swollen. She was spent and her head throbbed. It'd been a long day. So much had happened. Plus, she'd travelled by train, plane, bus, boat then car. If she could find a horse, she'd be able to cross every mode of transportation off her list in one day, but she was too tired to go looking for one.

* * *

The next morning, she rose early feeling much better. The sore throat was gone, and the headache too. As she walked down the stairs to the kitchen for breakfast, she felt well rested and eager to see the cottage and how much progress Brett had made while she was gone.

Dani was at the table eating a bowl of cereal. She wore athletic gear, and her cheeks were bright red.

Bea kissed the top of her head. "Hi, honey. Already been for a run, have you?"

Dani grinned around a mouthful, chewed and swallowed.

"I'm glad you're back, Mum, but I wish you and Dad could've worked things out. I'm assuming this means you won't?"

Bea slumped into a chair beside her. "Sorry, honey, it doesn't look like it. I know you wanted that for us, but we tried."

Dani's face clouded briefly. "That's okay. We'll figure out a way to be a family. I want you to be happy more than anything."

"I know you do. And I'm excited to see where you're up to with the cottage. How does it look?"

Dani's eyes sparkled. "It's almost done. I can't wait to show you. We've got a few touch-ups to do here and there. I can't believe how quickly they've worked, but Brett said it's such a small job that he needed it done fast so they could progress to their next, much bigger job."

"Good for us!"

They finished breakfast and got dressed. Bea wore shorts and a t-shirt with a hoodie tied around her waist. There was a cool breeze. Nothing like the one that cut right through her coat in Sydney. Even though it was spring it was overcast, and the usually cheerful sun was hidden behind low-hung clouds. The wind whipped the ocean into small white tufts of froth. They drove the old station wagon down the narrow winding track to the edge of the beach.

Bea was surprised to see Aidan's truck parked next to the cottage. The landscaping was almost complete, with a patch of turf and a few small mulched garden beds holding hardy Australian shrubbery. There was a short gravel path leading up to the front porch. But no sign of Aidan.

"Wow. It looks amazing," Bea gushed, climbing out of the car.

"Wait until you see inside," Dani said, her brown eyes crinkling at the edges as she ushered Bea along the path.

The kitchen was first — the marble bench tops were stunning in white with grey and black flecks. The white cabinetry with a Hamptons-style finish was perfectly suited to the beach setting. As was the light blue floral wallpaper with the tiny yellow flowers.

"I love it. It's come together so beautifully."

"I think so too," Dani agreed.

When Bea stepped into the living room, she saw Aidan standing on a stepladder adjusting a framed portrait of her with Dani and Harry.

He glanced over his shoulder and climbed down from the ladder, then raised his arms in the air. "Ta da! What do you think?"

Her throat tightened. It was amazing. There were photographs and pieces of artwork hung on every wall in matching timber frames. Pictures of her family and of the beach as well as some colourful artistic prints she'd never seen before. The room was unfurnished, but the space had been completely transformed with freshly installed timber flooring, white walls and new light fixtures. The photographs completed the look and brought tears to her eyes.

"You did this?" she asked, her voice catching.

He nodded. "Dani helped me get the photos, and she did the artwork."

"What?" She glanced at Dani, whose cheeks flushed pink. "You did this?"

Dani shrugged. "I like playing around on my laptop."

She pressed both hands to her chest. "It's breathtaking. I couldn't have asked for anything more. Thank you for this. You are so talented. I mean, I knew that, but seeing how far you've come... wow."

Dani grinned. "It was fun."

"You have a gift, honey." Bea kissed Dani's cheek and wrapped an arm around her shoulders as she continued to admire the room.

"That's what I told her as well," Aidan said, hands on hips as he studied one of the pieces of art — an asymmetric mixture of colours that reminded Bea of the beach outside the cottage's front door.

"And thank you for the coffee maker, Aidan — you didn't have to do that, but I'm very grateful you did."

He beamed. "I'm glad you like it. I wanted to do something to make your move-in day special."

"Move-in day?" Bea spun to face Dani, her brow furrowed.

Dani laughed. "I've already packed up most of our things. We're moving in!"

"What about furniture?"

"We don't need furniture." Dani linked an arm through Bea's. "We'll make do with air mattresses until our things arrive from Sydney."

"I don't know what to say." Bea was breathless. This was so much better than anything she'd pictured in her head. It was perfect.

"Say yes! Let's do it!" Dani grinned.

"Yes! Let's do it!" Bea replied.

She threw her arms around her daughter again and hugged her tight. "Thank you, honey. You don't know how much this whole thing means to me. It's everything I could've hoped for, and I'm sorry I wasn't here to help you more."

Dani waved her off. "You started the ball rolling, and I'm not sure I would've had the confidence to do that without you. I've loved the whole process. I wanted to tell you this in person, I've been keeping it to myself. But you'll be living here alone — I've re-enrolled at university. I'm going to study interior design. No more social work for me."

"Design? Are you sure?"

"I think so. This project helped me come alive. I didn't realise how much I love managing a design project until now.

This was fulfilling and exciting, and I can imagine myself doing it every day for a living."

Knowing her daughter had found something that made her happy shifted an enormously heavy burden that'd rested on Bea's shoulders for months. She sighed. "I'm thrilled, honey."

"You're not upset that I'll be leaving?"

Bea cupped Dani's cheek. "I wouldn't want it any other way. It's time for you to fly off and live your life. Knowing that you're happy, healthy and doing something you love will be all the company I need."

"I'm glad to hear it because I leave in two weeks. I've already begun the course online, but I have to get back to Sydney to attend in-person classes."

Bea tried not to show her shock. She'd wanted to live in the cottage with Dani for longer than that. It'd been a dream she'd allowed herself to foster over the past months since leaving Sydney. But returning to university was what Dani needed to do in order to find her place in the world, and Bea would never get in the way of that. In fact, she'd do anything to help either one of her children find their bliss. "I'll miss you. But I'm excited for you as well."

Dani left to get some bags from the car, and Bea wandered over to where Aidan was hanging another photograph. "These are so great. Thank you for all your hard work. I can't believe how thoughtful you've been. It means a lot to me."

He climbed down from the stepladder and met her gaze. "You're welcome. Are you going to be okay living here on your own? I seem to remember a time when you were afraid of snakes and spiders and couldn't bear the idea of being alone in a house at night."

She laughed. "That was a long time ago. I'm not a little girl anymore."

His eyes sparked. "No, you're not. Have you seen the coffee maker yet?"

She clapped her hands together. "Oh, I forgot. Real coffee — I may never leave this cottage again in my life. It's absolutely perfect."

He followed her into the kitchen. "You'll have to leave at some point if you intend to run a café. Are you still going to do that? I wasn't sure what your plans were, or if you were even coming back for a while there."

She turned the dials on the coffee machine in silence for a few moments, then faced him. "I'll be honest—I wasn't sure if I was coming back either. As you know, I wanted to work on my relationship with my husband, and he assured me that's what he wanted as well. But it seems his efforts were less than genuine and that he wasn't prepared to give up his fiancée the way he'd promised me he would."

"I'm sorry. That must've been hard."

She shrugged. "Not as hard as I thought it would be. It was actually a relief to get back here to the island and to my real life, as I've come to think of it."

"Your real life?"

"With the people I care about. Of course, I hated to leave Harry behind, but he's happy where he is, and he's promised to visit in the holidays."

"So, you're staying, then?"

She nodded. "I'm staying. There's nowhere else I'd rather be."

Nineteen

❧

BEA AND DANI spent their first night at the cottage on air mattresses. Bea's mattress deflated at two a.m., and she spent the rest of the night rolling from side to side trying to get comfortable. She awoke early with a crick in her neck and sciatica in one hip.

A hot shower helped her neck to loosen up a little bit, but she still walked with a limp. Breakfast was a cold croissant with jam and a hot cup of tea as she perched on a fallen log outside the cottage. The log was uncomfortable, but the view was worth it.

Something scampered across her hand where it rested on the log, and she squealed as she leapt to her feet. A spider went flying onto the sand in the dim light of dawn. She jogged in place, shaking her hands up and down as she continued emitting something halfway between a squeal and a groan.

"Ugh, I hate spiders."

She'd never been good with the creepy crawly creatures. When she was a kid, she'd had nightmares about them, and Dad had promised to kill any that came near her. Then she was married and Preston would take care of it with a stomp of

183

one shoe. But now that she and Dani lived alone, it would be up to her to deal with spiders, and she wasn't sure that was something she was ready to do. Perhaps she could convince Dani to take on the role of spider killer. But then Dani would leave and she'd have to face it alone.

As she hobbled down to the beach to watch the sunrise, the tension in her hip gradually eased until she was walking normally. She soon forgot all about the spider, although her hand continued to tingle for a few more minutes where its tiny feet had scrambled over her skin.

It was her back that caused the most discomfort. She'd have to find a much better solution than an air mattress if she was going to live at the cottage before her furniture arrived. Maybe the local op shop would have something secondhand she could use, or there could be something in Dad's basement that she'd forgotten.

She increased her pace to stride along the beach, enjoying the fresh air as it filled her lungs and the feel of the cold sand beneath the soles of her feet. There was no wind blowing at this time of day, and the sounds of the island coming into wakefulness filled the silence.

Birds squawked and twittered, diving for early morning insects all along the dunes and into the forest beyond. Somewhere nearby, an engine roared along a road and someone hammered a nail into place — the sound echoing dully through the still air.

There was movement at the edge of the sand, but since the dunes were still bathed in a semi-darkness, she couldn't quite see what it was. She changed course and headed up the beach to take a closer look. The creature was dark in colour and moved slowly through the white sand.

As she drew near, she saw that it was a small pademelon, one of the tiny marsupials that populated Coral Island. They looked like a wallaby with their soft brownish-grey fur, pointed ears, long hind feet and long tails. This one was tiny and clearly a juvenile. It appeared to be having difficulty hopping.

Bea moved closer and spoke in a soothing voice. "I'm not going to hurt you, little one. Let me take a look and see what's wrong. You've cut your foot on something, have you?"

She couldn't tell the extent of the damage from where she stood but knew she'd have to do something to help the creature. It wouldn't last long in the wild if it was unable to find food or escape predators. There were very few predators on the island. The small number of domesticated cats and dogs who lived there, posed the biggest threat to the local wildlife.

"I'm going to get a towel, and I'll be back in a moment," she told the creature.

She hurried as fast as she could manage back to the cottage. She was puffing hard by the time she reached it. Dani was awake and seated on the kitchen bench, halfway through a piece of toast with Vegemite on it.

"We don't have a fridge," she mumbled. "And I need milk for my coffee."

Bea laughed. "You'll have to go to Dad's for that until our fridge arrives. I think it's coming tomorrow. By the way, I've found an injured pademelon on the beach. I'm going to put it in the car and drive to the animal sanctuary with it."

"Oh, okay. Do you need help?"

"No, I'm fine."

Just then, a truck pulled into the driveway and parked. Bea peered through the kitchen window to see Aidan climbing out of the cab. She walked out to greet him.

"Good morning. Fancy seeing you here. You do know that it's only just after dawn, don't you?"

He laughed and held up three travel coffee cups. "I thought you might need help until you get all the ingredients for coffee at your house."

She shook her head. "You are an absolute lifesaver. Dani will be over the moon."

Dani rushed past her to grab one of the cups. "It's like you're a mind reader. Thank you, thank you, thank you!"

He laughed as Dani took a sip then headed back into the house, still in her pyjamas. "You're the best, Aidan! I mean it."

"I think you've won her over," Bea said, taking the coffee cup Aidan offered her.

"And how about you?"

Her heart thudded. Was he flirting with her? She was so out of practice, she couldn't be sure. "Definitely a fan."

She drank from her coffee cup and let her eyes drift shut as the flavour filled her mouth and the hot beverage ran down her throat. "That is divine. Oh, hang on. I've got something I have to do fairly urgently. I don't mean to be rude, but I have to go."

She raced back into the house, found a towel and headed out the back door.

Aidan followed. "Can I help you with anything?"

She nodded. "That would be fantastic. How are you at catching wildlife?"

He fell into step beside her. "What's going on?"

"There's an injured pademelon on the beach. I thought I'd take the poor thing to the sanctuary and see if Penny can do something to help it."

"Ah, okay. Let's see if we can catch it, then."

They found the animal only a little way from where Bea had left it earlier. She threw the towel over it, and Aidan scooped it up into his arms and held it as gently as possible while they strode back to his truck. Bea told Dani goodbye and joined Aidan to drive to the Coral Island Wildlife Rescue Centre. It was on the eastern side of the island in the middle of nowhere and it took them half an hour to drive there.

A small cluster of homes ran along the beach beside it, a

tiny village looking out over the ocean. The locals called it St James, after Penny's family. They were the first to build there, from what Bea could remember. She'd spent several sleepovers in the family beach house during her school years.

"I can't wait to see what Penny's done with the sanctuary," Bea said.

"She came home from living overseas after a breakup, I believe. She built a wildlife sanctuary on the land next to their beach house and from what I've heard, it's top notch. How's the patient?"

Bea peeked through a gap in the towel to see the animal resting in her lap. "Seems fine."

"The towel was a good idea."

"I think it's exhausted as well. Possibly lost a lot of blood. I guess we'll find out soon."

When they pulled into the parking lot beside the wildlife sanctuary, Bea climbed out and carried the injured pademelon in her arms to the side gate. The sanctuary was surrounded by a tall wire fence, and there was a white building inside the fence. Aidan pressed the buzzer by the gate, and after a while, Penny appeared to unlock it.

"Beatrice! What a pleasant surprise," she said. "Hello, Aidan. Fancy seeing the two of you here together."

Penny offered Bea a wink, which she studiously ignored while her cheeks blazed. "We brought an injured animal."

"Let's take a look, then." Penny opened the towel and studied the creature for a moment then covered it back up. "Come with me. We'll get set up in the clinic and find out what's going on. Evie will be thrilled. She just popped over to see me for a cup of tea. She volunteers every now and then so we can catch up."

"What good timing," Bea said.

Aidan followed the two of them as they walked through the sanctuary. There were large cages holding all different types of native animals. The cages were clean and filled with branches and leaves, so it was often difficult to see the occupants. Penny pushed through a door and into the building, then led them down a short hall and into a room that looked like a surgery apart from the small cages filled with animals — some sleeping, others bandaged.

A young woman stood at a bench, a pair of glasses perched on the end of her nose as she ran her finger over a piece of paper in front of her.

"Hi, Anna. This is Beatrice and Aidan, and they've brought us a patient."

Anna greeted them then checked on the pademelon. "Oh, she's beautiful."

"Can you please clean her up so we can get a better idea of what's going on with her?"

"Sure thing," Anna said.

"Let's go and see Evie, and I'll make you each a cup of tea."

They found Evie seated at a small round table in the kitchen beside a plate of chocolate biscuits and fresh sliced fruit. A kettle boiled on the bench behind her, whistling a trail of steam that rose high above it.

She looked up and smiled. "I was about to call you."

"Oh?" Bea embraced her and sat beside her, reaching for a chocolate biscuit.

Aidan sat as well and took a slice of apple from the pile of fruit. He leaned towards Bea, and the heat of his body sent a thrill through her. She loved that he was with her, that they were spending so much time together. Her biggest concern was that she needed more time to put her marriage behind her, to get over the hurt her husband had caused her.

The last thing she wanted to do was move on before she was ready and cause Aidan any pain. They'd already broken each other's hearts all those years ago. She didn't want to go through that again or put him through it either. They should be friends for now. Nothing more than that. Time would help them both understand whether there was more between them than history and affection.

"I've got your photographs with me. A copy, anyway. I was going to drop them by your place later, but I brought them over for Penny to take a look."

Penny sat and grabbed a handful of grapes from the plate. "I haven't seen them yet, and I still don't know why you think it will mean anything to me. I was neither born nor a baby when they were hidden in the wall. I have no idea what's in them or why someone would hide them in Bea's cottage."

Evie grinned. "You'll see."

"You're being very cryptic," Aidan said.

Evie pulled a yellow envelope out of her purse and set it on the table. She tugged a series of enlarged photographs from the envelope and spread them out in front of her. They were grainy and discoloured. All in black and white, but with a brownish hue.

Bea leaned forward, and her eyes narrowed. "Is that your beach house, Penny?" She pointed to a photograph of a man and woman standing on a porch with two children in front of them. All four squinted at the camera. An older woman stood off to one side looking at them instead of the camera.

They were dressed for the beach, but in the post-war style. Shorts and buttoned shirts for the man and the boy, a floral buttoned dress and straw hat for the woman, and a one-piece swimsuit for the little girl, whose curls were caught blowing above her head, her lips pulled into a broad smile.

Penny studied the image. "Yes, that's definitely my beach house. How funny. Who are these people, though?"

"I don't know," Bea said as she looked through the other images. "Here they are again." The photographs seemed to be of the same family. Some were posed, with the family seated inside.

Others captured moments in time when the family was in the middle of doing something and were stopped by the picture taker to capture the verve of their lives. There were even a couple where the photographer had attempted to take an action shot on the beach, but the figures were blurred, as were the waves and several seagulls in mid-flight.

"I wonder why they hid these photos in a wall," Aidan said.

"Who knows?" Evie replied.

"They look vaguely familiar, don't they? Who owned the place before your parents bought it, Penny?"

"Do you know old June Clements, the woman who runs the Kellyville Bakery?" Penny asked.

Bea nodded. "Of course. I saw her again when I first arrived on the island. She was very amused that I wanted to order a croissant."

"It was her parents who owned the place. They built it before the war. I vaguely remember them, but by the time I came along, they were mostly out of the picture. No pun intended." She grinned and pointed at the photographs. "But those *other* people are my mum, my step-dad, and my grandmother."

Aidan picked one up. "Didn't your family have some kind of tragedy there?"

"That's right," Penny agreed. "My grandmother was killed and they never caught her murderer. Mum and Dad always said the place was haunted after that."

"I still can't believe that happened on our quiet little island."

"It was a long time ago. I didn't know my grandmother," Penny said.

"*Is* it haunted?" Evie asked.

"Not unless you include the python that lives in the roof," Penny replied.

Bea shuddered. "Ugh, how can you stay there?"

"Monty keeps the rat population down for me."

"I'll never get used to that," Bea replied.

Evie got up to make cups of tea, asking everyone what they wanted while she worked. Bea studied the photographs again, racking her brain to remember anything she could about the Clements family and the murder that'd become a kind of urban legend on the island since.

"There was a boy at school with us, Rowan Clements..." Bea said.

"He was a nasty boy." Penny wrinkled her nose.

"Why is that?" Evie asked as she set tea cups down in front of them.

"He bullied me constantly. Never left me alone about my curly hair, my freckles, my bony knees... Anything he could think of to point out as a flaw, he latched on and wouldn't let it go."

Bea arched her eyebrows. "I remember that. It's all coming back to me. Funny how you forget about things that happened until someone reminds you. I could've sworn there was no bullying at our school, but now you say that, it's as though you've found the key to a lockbox of memories in my mind and it's been flung open."

"I wonder where Rowan Clements is now," Evie said.

Aidan bit into a biscuit. " We've caught up a few times over the years. Last I heard, he was working in the States as a journalist."

"What?"

"A pretty good one, too. I see him occasionally when I'm watching the news."

"Yes, and it's quite the leap for a boy who used to eat his

own boogers," Penny snipped. "He's still friends with Rob, although I don't know what my brother sees in him."

"I suppose we've all changed," Bea said. She glanced up at Aidan, who met her gaze with a quizzical look as though her words held a kind of hidden meaning.

"Yes, we have," he said. "And perhaps we should give Rowan the benefit of the doubt. After all, everyone deserves a second chance. Don't they?" A smile teased the corners of his mouth, and his eyes crinkled at the edges.

The intensity of his gaze brought goose pimples to Bea's arms, and she folded them to hide her reaction. She needed to maintain a distance from Aidan Whitlock for a while or she wouldn't be able to keep her emotions in check. Remaining friends was going to be more difficult than she'd thought it would be.

Twenty

THE WEATHER WAS HEATING up every single day that passed. Winter was brief and mild on the island and had disappeared months earlier. Spring raced by with a whiff of pollen in the air. And now Summer had already begun, and the feel of heat hung in the atmosphere from the early morning hours like a fog.

The island smelled of beaches and swimming, visits to the waterfall and diving into the stream to frolic in the cool darkness as the water pounded them from overhead. Summer brought back memories of fishing and diving, snorkelling and bonfires at night as they fried their catch on an open fire and sat in the sand talking for hours about what life might look like when they got their freedom.

It was a million different dreams from childhood for Bea. Memories she'd left behind long ago and hadn't taken out to sift through much since because those memories also carried with them images of her mother, laughing and crying, singing and dancing, and the pain of losing her so early in life.

Bea thought of all those things while lying on the old mattress she'd lugged down from her father's basement to put into the cottage the previous day. It'd worked better overnight than the air mattress. It smelled of dank mould and mustiness, but she supposed beggars couldn't be choosers.

Penny's team had fixed the little pademelon up with a few stitches and some food and water. Apparently something had attacked it, possibly a cat or dog. But it was recovering at the wildlife refuge, and Penny had promised to keep Bea up-to-date with its progress.

She climbed out of bed with a yawn, her mind already running over the list of things she had to achieve that day and the discussion she'd had the previous morning with her friends about the photographs. She'd brought the pictures home with her and had them laid out on the kitchen bench. Then, she'd settled down to study them while she made herself a cup of coffee.

The movers had brought her things from the Sydney storage facility the day before. And she'd spent the rest of the day unpacking and had a few items of furniture positioned around the place, including an armchair she'd bought at a local boutique a few days earlier.

The rest of her belongings were still in boxes outside on the porch. She'd work on positioning more things around the place later, including her king-sized bed that they'd dismantled and set in pieces against her bedroom wall. She couldn't wait to get rid of the stinky mattress. The cottage was fast becoming a home.

Bea took her time soaking in a hot bath. The view of the beach through her one-way window was breathtaking, and she was entirely relaxed by the time it was over. She put on a summer dress and decided to let her hair dry naturally, then sat on the porch with a book while the sun crept up the beach and into her garden. The unpacking could wait a little longer. She had nothing but time.

When Dad and Bradford arrived later, she was ready to go

with them to see her new café. She'd already signed the contract with Evie, and she needed to get back to Brett regarding the work she wanted done. She was glad she could use the same contractor as she had for the cottage, since he'd done such a good job and worked quickly. He had sent her a quote as well as some advice after his initial walk-through a few weeks prior. Today was all about finalising her needs so he could get started.

"Hi, Dad," she said, rising from her rocking chair. She closed the book and set it on a small table. "How was fishing this morning, Brad?"

Bradford's hair was dishevelled, and he looked as though he hadn't slept much. "I got up far too early, and nothing was biting."

"That's frustrating."

"Tell me about it. I'm looking forward to seeing your café, though. Dad tells me it's gonna be a great little business."

Anxiety and anticipation twisted Bea's gut. "I think so, but I suppose we'll see soon enough. It's a big risk, so I'm feeling a little nervous about it. But I also think it will be a good investment."

"Let's go, then," Bradford said.

Dad opened the car door for her, and she slid into the back seat. They rode together to Kellyville with the windows down and the radio on. Bea sang along to the music, and soon Dad and Bradford joined in. She beamed all the way there. It was like old times again. She could almost imagine Bradford's braces on his crooked teeth and her soccer cleats on her feet.

They'd shared a lot of good times when they were children, but for some reason, they'd both let the pain of their loss cloud those memories. They should talk more about the laughter, the fun, the happiness they'd shared. Perhaps then they'd actually enjoy spending time together more often.

They walked around the space for an hour while Bea

wrote in a small notepad all the things they identified to fix. There was a brand-new kitchen to install, along with everything from new stovetop, ovens and pizza oven. She wanted all stainless-steel benches and an extension on the walk-in refrigerator. The rest of the café was in good shape and needed only a fresh coat of paint, new furnishings and decorative touches.

There was also a small outdoor seating area that she envisioned with wrought iron chairs, tables and climbing ivy filled with twinkle lights. Her imagination was in overdrive putting together the look, feel and especially menu for her new venture, and by the time they'd finished the walk-through, she was buzzing with excitement.

They all sat on the steps outside the café. Bradford had taken photographs and ran through them on his camera screen while Bea finished taking notes. Dad sat in silence, as was his tendency, and gazed out over the nearby marina, where a group of pelicans fought over something — no doubt a piece of fish left behind by a fisherman. The largest pelican gulped the prize down and waddled off with a satisfied squawk.

"You think you can manage all this?" Dad asked.

Bea set down her pen and looked around. "I think so. I've run a semi-successful catering company out of my house, plus lots of events, Parent Teacher Association fundraisers and Athletic Club functions. This should be a walk in the park compared to that." She laughed, but the laughter did little to mask her anxiety.

The truth was, she wasn't sure she could manage anything at all. The divorce had undermined the last of her self-confidence, and she did what she could to pretend everything was fine, but beneath the surface, she couldn't help wondering if she was good enough.

"Of course she can," Bradford said, putting his camera away in its bag. "She's amazing. She can do anything."

"Thanks, Brad," she said. "I wonder what Mum would've thought of something like this."

Brad met her gaze. "She would've loved it. But you know that."

"I guess so. Sometimes it's hard to remember what she was really like. I get confused about whether I'm remembering the version of her I want to remember or the person she really was."

He shrugged. "I guess we all do that a little bit."

"Because the fact is, she was pretty difficult a lot of the time."

Dad sighed. "We like to recall the good in people after they're gone. Nothing wrong with that. I'm going to check out the garden shed in the back—see what they've got stored out there. Might even be a generator if we're lucky."

Bea handed him the keys, and he wandered off.

"He doesn't like talking about Mum," Bradford explained.

Bea frowned. "I know that. I know Dad too, in case you've forgotten."

Bradford's nostrils flared. "You haven't exactly been present lately."

"I'm here now, aren't I?"

"Yes, but there have been a lot of years in between."

"Excuse me for having a family and giving them my atten-tion," she spat. Even as she heard the words come from her mouth, she didn't understand why she was being so harsh with Brad. He was her brother. She loved and admired him. He was one of her favourite people in the whole world, and yet he pushed her buttons in a way no one else could.

"What are you saying, Bea? It's not my fault I don't have a family."

She stood to her feet and pressed her hands to her hips. "Maybe you're here out of guilt, but I'm here because I love Dad and this island."

"Guilt?" He stood as well, glowering at her. "Here we go again. You're still blaming me for Mum's death, aren't you?"

She huffed. "Would it have been so hard for you to be a decent son?"

"I was a teen boy, Bea," he growled. "It's not fair to blame a child for a grown woman's choices. I've blamed myself for enough years, but I've been through therapy and worked out that it wasn't my fault."

The wind was sucked from Bea's lungs as her old arguments and all her rage over her mother's death collapsed. The reality was she blamed herself, not him. But she'd taken it out on him.

She inhaled a slow breath. "I'm sorry, Brad. You're right. Of course it wasn't your fault. I was angry. She had everything to live for. I had to find a reason for her to leave us because if it wasn't your fault, I guess I was scared that it was mine."

Bea pressed both hands to her face. Bradford wrapped her up in his arms. She leaned against his chest.

"It's okay," he said. "I was a difficult kid — I couldn't control my emotions. I wanted to push the boundaries and have fun with my friends. But when she chose to take her own life and leave us alone like that, it only made me sad. I couldn't get angry about it for a long time. It was only when I started asking myself why that the rage took over, and by then, you'd already left home. I spent years chasing answers at the bottom of a bottle or doing crazy things like diving out of planes. But now I know—she made her choices, and I'm only responsible for mine."

"How did you get so wise?" She slapped him playfully on the shoulder. "I'm supposed to be the big sister."

He shrugged. "I guess I've spent decades dealing with it while you've been busy raising kids. They're great, by the way. Your kids are amazing. You should be proud."

"Thanks. I think they're pretty wonderful, although I'm

not sure it's anything to do with me. They came out that way."

He laughed. "You've done well, Bea. And this café is just what you need to make a fresh start."

* * *

That night, Bea got ready for her first official date with Aidan. Actually, she wasn't certain it was a date. She wasn't sure what to think at all. From her perspective, the two of them had an unspoken agreement that they would be friends. He was a famous ex-footballer, she was a newly divorced, suburban mum with so much baggage that she'd had to rent a storage facility. The fact that they'd had a relationship in high school and he was her first love and she was his, complicated things, but it didn't change the facts.

He'd called earlier in the afternoon and asked if she'd like to go out to dinner at the restaurant on the pier called *Surf and Sea*. It was her favourite seafood restaurant on the island and had been around ever since she was a child.

She and Aidan used to sit outside and watch all the adults in their best outfits walking into the restaurant on dates and nights out and dream that one day they'd be able to afford to eat there.

She donned a little black dress and a light wrap, then curled her hair and applied makeup. She'd decided that their first date, if it was even that, at *Surf and Sea* deserved a little extra effort. When he arrived promptly at seven, she was almost ready. He made small talk with Dani, Dad and Bradford in the living room while she finished up, then she walked down the stairs in her high heels to meet him.

He looked up at her, a sheepish smile on his face, cheeks rosy. He wore a button-down shirt in light blue and a pair of dark blue jeans. He was the most handsome man she'd ever known, and he'd only improved with age. She couldn't believe it was her reflection gleaming in his ocean-coloured eyes.

He held out a hand for her, and she took it when she reached the bottom of the staircase.

"You look beautiful, Bumble Bea," he said.

"Right back at you."

Aidan's eyes flitted to the floor, and he stepped forward and stomped.

Bea startled. "What on earth?"

"Spider," he said. "Don't worry—it's not coming back from that." He laughed and held out his arm for her to take.

Bea's heart skipped a beat. "My hero."

She slipped a hand through the crook of his arm and together they said goodbye to Dad and Dani.

Outside, she looked around in confusion. "Where's your truck?"

He was still holding her hand. It felt warm, natural and completely surreal. As though she'd stepped back in time. But this man beside her was no seventeen-year-old boy — skinny, awkward and unsure of himself. He was strong, confident and complete. She could see that now. He'd grown and changed. He wasn't going to second-guess his choices the way he'd done back then. She could trust him with her heart.

"I didn't bring the truck," he said. "How do you feel about traveling by boat?"

Her eyes widened. "I should've worn a different outfit."

"You'll be fine. I brought a blanket."

"I'll grab a scarf for my hair and be right back." She hurried inside and pulled a silk scarf off the coat rack where she'd hung it after the last time she'd travelled to the island on the ferry, then tied it quickly over her curled hair in the hall mirror.

Outside, Aidan took her hand again and led her down the winding path in front of the house to the beach below. She had to slip her heels off and carry them in her hand. The sand and grass were cool and soft beneath her feet. His small boat waited beside a large black rock. She clambered up the rock and into the boat, with his hand guiding her the entire way. Then he climbed in and secured the anchor, and they were off.

Being out on the water in the last of the twilight was exhilarating. The sunset was a spectacular orange with yellow shafts of light glinting on the ocean's surface. The boat surged up and over every small wave. She wrapped the blanket around her legs and sat back to enjoy the ride.

Aidan stood tall and straight at the steering wheel. His broad shoulders flexed as he turned the wheel to head out of the bay and around the point. Bea looked up at the stars overhead. They were coming to life one by one in the darkening sky. Soon they would be innumerable, but for now, there were only a few and she wondered about them, where they were, how far away and what they would look like up close.

Living on the island again had brought her out of the busyness of her city life and gave her a chance to ponder, to dream and to wonder in a way that she hadn't done in years. When they arrived at the dock, Aidan tied up the boat and helped Bea out. She slipped her shoes back on and walked to the restaurant with her arm looped through his.

Before they reached the door, she pulled him aside.

He faced her, one brow quirked. "Is everything okay?"

"Before we go in there, I need to talk to you about something."

His eyes narrowed. "Okay."

It was almost entirely dark. The moon was large and bright, leaving a long reflective trail across the water. And from the restaurant wafted delicious scents and the sound of light jazz music, along with laughter and conversation.

"Why did you pick this restaurant?"

He shrugged. "You know why."

"I'd like you to say it."

"Because when we were kids, we used to sit on that dock, feeding the pelicans and dreaming that one day we'd get to dress up fancy and eat here. We never got the chance because we broke up before either one of us was an adult or had the money to pay the bill. So, I wanted to do this for you, for us."

His words brought a lump to her throat. "Thank you."

He grinned. "You're welcome." He went to move, but she tugged him to a stop again.

"I don't want to rush anything."

He rested his hands on her shoulders and looked down into her eyes. "I don't either."

"Because I've just come through a divorce, the ink is still fresh, and I'm not ready."

"I understand."

"I don't want you to think I don't care about you. I do."

"That's good to know. I appreciate the heads-up." He smiled.

They went inside the restaurant and found their reserved seats. Soft jazz music played in the background. Candlelight flickered against the walls and Bea was heady with the feel of Aidan's hand at her waist as he guided her to the table, the way his eyes sparkled in the golden light and the sense of excitement that coursed through her veins.

She was on a date — hadn't been on one in decades. It felt decadent, sensual and completely forbidden. She didn't know what to do with herself — where to lay her hand, how to speak, what to order.

In the end, she settled on a serving of barramundi in lemon and butter sauce, with a side of fresh vegetables and *pomme frites*. Aidan ordered the crab dish, and they chatted amicably while they waited for the food to be delivered to their table.

"Did you ever imagine we'd end up here again someday?" Bea asked with a smile as she reached for a piece of bread.

"When my wife died, the pain of grief overwhelmed me again, and I realised then how much you must've gone through when you lost your mother. It helped me to understand you better than I had at the time. I've wanted to say this for a long time: I'm sorry."

"Thank you." His words touched her heart.

"I never had a family — I had my wife, and we were mostly happy together. Although there were times we struggled and we almost split up once or twice. Both of us longed to have children, a family. I missed out on that. But when I'm with you — it feels like family to me. We have so much history together." He grinned. "You fit my compulsive, overly organised, perfectionist self. You ground me, you keep things real, you're kind and thoughtful, and you always put other people's needs ahead of your own."

She swallowed. "Maybe you're confusing me with another girlfriend. Your university sweetheart, perhaps? Did she also have blonde hair and dimples in her cheeks?"

He threw back his head and laughed. "And you're funny, too."

"I love that you've thought this through."

"But you still want to take it slow..." he said.

She nodded. "When Preston left me, in some ways it was unexpected, but in other ways it wasn't. I can look back now and see how far we'd drifted apart over the years, but I was in denial. I'm not sure my heart can be repaired from the damage he caused."

He reached a hand across the table and took Bea's in his. The warmth of his touch sent a bolt of lightning through her. "You were the one for me. You always have been. I know that now. Sometimes all we need is a second chance at first love."

First love. The words washed over her like a balm. He'd

been her first love, and she was his. Love like that wasn't easily forgotten, but so much had happened since then. "I don't want to hurt you."

"You won't hurt me," he said. "And I'll wait for you as long as it takes. I'm not going anywhere."

* * *

A week later, Bea arranged for a group of friends to come to the cottage for a party and a bonfire on the beach as a send-off for Dani, who was headed back to Sydney the next day to attend university. Bea and Dani spent the day cooking, cleaning and packing up Dani's things. They'd managed to go to Airlie Beach the previous weekend to buy a few items of outdoor furniture, but had asked the guests to bring chairs since nothing had been delivered yet.

Bea made slow-cooked chicken and sliced up all the toppings needed for tacos and nachos. Dani made cheesecake and pavlova for dessert, to be served with fresh whipped cream.

When Penny arrived, she brought a large container of sliced watermelon which Bea added to the table. Then, Penny got to work setting up a self-serve bar.

Dad, Aidan and Bradford had arrived early to help build a bonfire on the beach. They'd collected a tower of sticks and driftwood and piled it up in a clump on the sand. Bea monitored their progress by speaking to her father on the two-way radio she'd gifted him until he was irritated with her interruptions and switched it off.

Evie arrived next, followed soon after by Taya. Bea had already set up the taco station as well as the drinks station on an outdoor table she'd borrowed from her father, so she sat with the other ladies around the newly lit bonfire.

It was a wonderful evening of good food, conversation and fun.

"How's it going with Aidan?" Evie asked as she set her plate of tacos in her lap.

Bea chewed a mouthful of nachos and swallowed. "It's good."

"Good, or really good?" Penny asked.

They all laughed. Taya wolf whistled.

"Wow, that was an impressive whistle," Bea said, covering her ears.

Taya winked. "I have a few hidden skills."

"What, like burping the national anthem?" Penny quipped.

Taya pretended to pout. "You said you'd keep that between us."

"Oh, come on. Now you have to show us," Bea shouted, laughing along with the others.

"Maybe later," Taya said. "We want to hear about Aidan. It's so romantic, the two of you getting back together after all these years. I just knew you were perfect for each other."

Bea's heart swelled. It did seem too good to be true. She could never have imagined she'd get a second chance to be loved by Aidan Whitlock. "We're taking things slowly."

"That's the best way," Penny said with a wink.

In the cottage, the sound of a bell ringing caught Bea's ear. "What on earth?" She stood and peered back through the darkness at the well-lit cottage.

Dani walked up the beach towards them. "I think that's the doorbell, Mum."

Bea huffed. "Who would ring the doorbell on a night like this? Just come around the back!" She yelled the last as loudly as she could manage.

Everyone fell quiet, waiting to see who it would be.

"Everyone I invited is already here," Bea mused.

A teenaged girl walked around the outside of the cottage on the wrap-around porch. She stood beneath the porch light, her brow furrowed. Bea didn't recognise her, so she hurried to meet her and find out what she wanted. The other ladies all followed.

"Hello!" she called as she puffed through the sand. "I'm Bea Rushton. Are you looking for me?"

The girl pressed her hands to her hips and studied Bea. "Actually, I was told Aidan Whitlock might be here. I tried his parents' house first, but they said he'd gone to a party on the beach and gave me directions."

Bea spun about and looked for Aidan. He was stoking the fire with a long, thin stick and talking to her brother. He threw his head back and laughed, and the golden light of the sunset glanced off his hair in a way that made him look gorgeous, young and carefree. It tugged at her heartstrings. If only she could put her past behind her and give herself over to loving him fully.

Two people finding each other again after so many years wasn't impossible. There was a good chance everything could work out between them. But her heart was still tender from her divorce, and she wasn't sure she was ready to take another chance so soon. She was grateful Aidan was willing to wait, to be patient. He'd had years to get over his own loss. He knew it would take her some time to get over hers too.

"There he is," she said, pointing.

The girl nodded. Her brows were drawn up towards the centre of her face as though she was concentrating on something very hard. She hesitated, then stepped forward and into the sand. She was young, maybe fourteen or fifteen years old, and thin, wearing a pair of shorts and a mismatched singlet top. Her hair was golden and wavy and fell halfway down her back. Her tanned legs pushed their way through the sand, and she leaned forward with the effort.

Bea watched her a moment, then trundled after her. She still wasn't sure who the girl was, but if she was a crazed football fan, perhaps Bea should follow and make sure the girl didn't spend the night attempting to garner autographs from Aidan. Although it seemed unlikely that someone so young would even know who Aidan was. He'd finished playing football five years earlier. Bea spun around to scan the parking area beside the cottage to see if the girl's parents had come with her.

She saw no sign of anyone waiting by a car and with a shrug turned to follow the girl, her friends falling into step beside her.

"Who is she?" asked Taya, puffing lightly as they walked.

"Not sure. She seems to know Aidan."

"What does she want?" asked Penny with a frown.

"I don't know."

"Funny that she's out here all alone when it's getting dark, don't you think?" Evie asked, tucking her red hair behind her ears.

"I guess. Unless she knows Aidan."

Evie arched an eyebrow. "I've never seen her before, though."

"She's not from the island?" Bea asked.

"No, I don't think so."

They all stopped a few feet away from the girl where she stood studying Aidan. He wasn't paying attention, still deep in conversation with Bradford.

"Excuse me. Aidan Whitlock?" the girl said, then cleared her throat with a cough.

Bea's suspicions grew. Clearly Aidan didn't know her at all. And she was behaving very strangely. She walked over to Aidan and stood beside him, watching his reaction.

He faced the girl, still smiling. "Yes. Can I help you?" Then he casually laced an arm around Bea's shoulders. She liked the way it felt, standing next to him, his arm around her pulling her in close. He smelled of aftershave and sea salt. His warmth set her skin tingling. A small bubble of joy welled in her stomach and worked its way up into her chest.

The girl's nostrils were flared and her cheeks flushed red. "Yes, I think you can. I'm your daughter."

Aidan froze, then his arm drifted off Bea's shoulders and down to his side. "What?"

"You're my dad," said the girl with a half shrug. "I'm Grace Allen. Pleased to meet you." She held out a hand as an awkward offering.

He took it as though numb and shook her hand slowly. "I don't understand."

"Surely you remember Kelly Allen?"

He grunted. "Uh, I guess so. It was a long time ago."

"Fifteen years ago, actually."

Bea looked up at Aidan, her eyes wide. His face was pale. He pushed his hands deep into the pockets of his shorts as a gasp went around the crowd of people standing there. Bea couldn't take it in. Surely this couldn't be real. Aidan was married fifteen years ago. He and his wife hadn't been able to have children. This made no sense at all. The girl must be lying.

"I've looked everywhere for you," the girl said. "Mum kicked me out. I need a place to stay. Can I stay with you, Dad? I've got nowhere else to go."

Aidan blinked. He glanced down at Bea. Her heart was in her throat. Questions poised, ready to leap from her tongue. Was this really happening? Did Aidan have a daughter?

* * *

Continue the series...

Ready to read book 2 in the *Coral Island* series so you can keep following Beatrice, Aidan and the

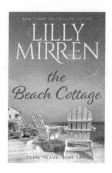

rest of the Coral Island crew? Buy the next book in this series!

Want to find out about all of my new releases? You can get on my VIP reader list by subscribing to my newsletter and you'll also get a free book.

Also by Lilly Mirren

WOMEN'S FICTION

CORAL ISLAND SERIES

The Island

After twenty five years of marriage and decades caring for her two children, on the evening of their vow renewal, her husband shocks her with the news that he's leaving her.

The Beach Cottage

Beatrice is speechless. It's something she never expected — a secret daughter. She and Aidan have only just renewed their romance, after decades apart, and he never mentioned a child. Did he know she existed?

The Blue Shoal Inn

Taya's inn is in trouble. Her father has built a fancy new resort in Blue Shoal and hired a handsome stranger to manage it. When the stranger offers to buy her inn and merge it with the resort, she wants to hate him but when he rescues a stray dog her feelings for him change.

Island Weddings

Charmaine moves to Coral Island and lands a job working at a local florist shop. It seems as though the entire island has caught wedding fever, with weddings planned every weekend. It's a good opportunity for her to get to know the locals, but what she doesn't expect is to be thrown into the middle of a family drama.

The Island Bookshop

Evie's book club friends are the people in the world she relies on most. But when one of the newer members finds herself confronted with her past, the rest of the club will do what they can to help, endangering the existence of the bookshop without realising it.

An Island Reunion

It's been thirty five years since the friends graduated from Coral Island State Primary School and the class is returning to the island to celebrate.

THE WARATAH INN SERIES

The Waratah Inn

Wrested back to Cabarita Beach by her grandmother's sudden death, Kate Summer discovers a mystery buried in the past that changes everything.

One Summer in Italy

Reeda leaves the Waratah Inn and returns to Sydney, her husband, and her thriving interior design business, only to find her marriage in tatters. She's lost sight of what she wants in life and can't recognise the person she's become.

The Summer Sisters

Set against the golden sands and crystal clear waters of Cabarita Beach three sisters inherit an inn and discover a mystery about their grandmother's past that changes everything they thought they knew about their family...

Christmas at The Waratah Inn

Liz Cranwell is divorced and alone at Christmas. When her friends convince her to holiday at The Waratah Inn, she's dreading her first Christmas on her own. Instead she discovers that strangers can be the balm to heal the wounds of a lonely heart in this heartwarming Christmas story.

EMERALD COVE SERIES

Cottage on Oceanview Lane

When a renowned book editor returns to her roots, she rediscovers her strength & her passion in this heartwarming novel.

Seaside Manor Bed & Breakfast

The Seaside Manor Bed and Breakfast has been an institution in Emerald Cove for as long as anyone can remember. But things are changing and Diana is nervous about what the future might hold for her and her husband, not to mention the historic business.

Bungalow on Pelican Way

Moving to the Cove gave Rebecca De Vries a place to hide from her abusive ex. Now that he's in jail, she can get back to living her life as a police officer in her adopted hometown working alongside her intractable but very attractive boss, Franklin.

Chalet on Cliffside Drive

At forty-four years of age, Ben Silver thought he'd never find love. When he moves to Emerald Cove, he does it to support his birth mother, Diana, after her husband's sudden death. But then he meets Vicky.

An Emerald Cove Christmas

The Flannigan family has been through a lot together. They've grown and changed over the years and now have a blended and extended family that doesn't always see eye to eye. But this Christmas they'll learn that love can overcome all of the pain and differences of the past in this inspiring Christmas tale.

MYSTERIES

White Picket Lies

Fighting the demons of her past Toni finds herself in the midst of a second marriage breakdown at forty seven years of age. She struggles to keep depression at bay while doing her best to raise a wayward teenaged son and uncover the identity of the killer.

In this small town investigation, it's only a matter of time until friends and neighbours turn on each other.

HISTORICAL FICTION (WRITING AS BRONWEN PRATLEY)

Beyond the Crushing Waves

An emotional standalone historical saga. Two children plucked from poverty & forcibly deported from the UK to

Australia. Inspired by true events. An unforgettable tale of loss, love, redemption & new beginnings.

Under a Sunburnt Sky

Inspired by a true story. Jan Kostanski is a normal Catholic boy in Warsaw when the nazis invade. He's separated from his neighbours, a Jewish family who he considers kin, by the ghetto wall. Jan and his mother decide that they will do whatever it takes to save their Jewish friends from certain death. The unforgettable tale of an everyday family's fight against evil, and the unbreakable bonds of their love.

Cast of Characters

As the *Coral Island* series grows, the cast of characters does too. I hope this handy reference will help.

* * *

Aidan Whitlock - former professional footballer, current primary school PE teacher.

Andrew Reddy - The new manager at *Paradise Resort.*

Annie Draper - Bea's friend from Sydney.

Beatrice Rushton - previously married and living in Sydney, now a resident of Coral Island.

Betsy Norton - Elderly, American, owns the florist shop.

Bradford Rushton - Bea's younger brother, owns a charter fishing company out of Airlie Beach.

Brett O'Hanley - Beatrice & Aidan's contractor.

Buck Clements - Rowan's step father and June's ex-husband.

Camden Futcher - Taya's adult daughter, training to become a chef in Cairns.

Cameron Eldridge - Taya's father and owner of *Paradise Resorts*.

Charmaine Billings - new resident of Coral Island, works at Betsy's Florals.

Danita Pike - Bea's adult daughter, lives in Sydney.

Elias Rushton - Bea's father, lives on Coral Island.

Eveleigh (Evie) Mair - Owner of *Eveleigh's Books*, the book shop attached the *Bea's Coffee*.

Frank Norton - Betsy's adult son and Samantha's father.

Fudge - Beatrice's pug.

Grace Allen - Aidan's teenaged daughter.

Harry Pike - Bea's adult son, lives in Sydney.

June Clements - proprietor of the *Coral Cafe* & Rowan's mother.

Kelly Allen - Grace's mother & Aidan's ex-girlfriend.

Luella Rushton - Bea's mother, deceased.

Mary Brown - Penny's grandmother, murder victim.

Ms Gossamer - librarian in Kellyville.

Penny St James - Owner of the Coral Island Wildlife Rescue centre.

Preston Pike - Bea's ex-husband, lives between Sydney & Melbourne.

Robert St James - Penny's brother, travels around to work in construction.

Rowan Clements - June Clements' son, journalist.

Ruby Brown - Penny's mother.

Samantha Norton - Betsy's granddaughter & Frank's daughter.

Taya Eldridge - Owns the Blue Shoal Inn, is Cameron & Tina Eldridge's daughter.

Tina Eldridge - Taya's mother, married to Cameron.

Todd Futcher - Taya's former husband, deceased.

About the Author

Lilly Mirren is an Amazon top 20, Audible top 15 and *USA Today* Bestselling author who has sold over two million copies of her books worldwide. She lives in Brisbane, Australia with her husband and three children.

Her books combine heartwarming storylines with realistic characters readers see as friends.

Her debut series, *The Waratah Inn*, set in the delightful Cabarita Beach, hit the *USA Today* Bestseller list and since then, has touched the hearts of hundreds of thousands of readers across the globe.